CHARLES BUKOWSKI

HOT WATER MUSIC

ecco
An Imprint of HarperCollinsPublishers

Previously published by Black Sparrow Press

HarperCollins books may be purchased for educational, business, or sales promotional use. For information, please e-mail the Special Markets Department at SPsales@harpercollins.com.

First Ecco edition published in 2002

The Library of Congress has catalogued a previous editions as follows:

Bukowski, Charles.1920-1994
  Hot water music.

  I. Title.
  PS3552.U4H6   1983   813'.54   86-15391
  ISBN 0-87685-597-4
  ISBN 0-87685-596-6 (pbk.)

24 25 26 27 28 LBC 49 48 47 46 45

for Michael Montfort

TABLE OF CONTENTS

Hot Water Music

LESS DELICATE THAN THE LOCUST

"Balls," he said, "I'm tired of painting. Let's go out. I'm tired of the stink of oils, I'm tired of being great. I'm tired of waiting to die. Let's go out."

"Go out where?" she asked.

"Anywhere. Eat, drink, see."

"Jorg," she said, "what will I do when you die?"

"You will eat, sleep, fuck, piss, shit, clothe yourself, walk around and bitch."

"I need security."

"We all do."

"I mean, we're not married. I won't even be able to collect your insurance."

"That's all right, don't worry about it. Besides, you don't believe in marriage, Arlene."

Arlene was sitting in the pink chair reading the afternoon newspaper. "You say five thousand women want to sleep with you. Where does that leave me?"

"Five thousand and one."

"You think I can't get another man?"

"No, there's no problem for you. You can get another man in three minutes."

"You think I need a great painter?"

"No, you don't. A good plumber would do."

"Yes, as long as he loved me."

"Of course. Put on your coat. Let's go out."

They came down the stairway from the top loft. All around were cheap, roach-filled rooms, but nobody seemed to be starving: they always seemed to be cooking things in large pots and sitting around, smoking, cleaning their fingernails, drinking cans of beer or sharing a tall blue bottle of white wine, screaming at each other or laughing, or farting, belching, scratching or asleep in front of the tv. Not many people in the world had very much money but the less money they had the better they seemed to live. Sleep, clean sheets, food, drink and hemorrhoid ointment were their only needs. And they always left their doors a bit open.

"Fools," said Jorg as they walked down the stairway, "they twaddle away their lives and clutter up mine."

"Oh, Jorg," Arlene sighed. "You just don't *like* people, do you?"

Jorg arched an eyebrow at her, didn't answer. Arlene's response to his feelings for the masses was always the same—as if not loving the people revealed an unforgivable shortcoming of soul. But she was an excellent fuck and pleasant to have around—most of the time.

They reached the boulevard and walked along, Jorg with his red and white beard and broken yellow teeth and bad breath, purple ears, frightened eyes, stinking torn overcoat and white ivory cane. When he felt worst he felt best. "Shit," he said, "everything shits until it dies."

Arlene bobbled her ass, making no secret of it, and Jorg pounded the pavement with his cane, and even the sun looked down and said, Ho ho. Finally they reached the old dingy building where Serge lived. Jorg and Serge had both been painting for many years but it was not until recently that their work sold for more than pig farts. They had starved together, now they were getting famous separately. Jorg and Arlene entered the hotel and began climbing the stairway. The smell of iodine and frying chicken was in the halls. In one room somebody was getting fucked and making no secret of it. They climbed to the top loft and Arlene knocked. The door popped open and there was Serge. "Peek-a-boo!" he said. Then he blushed. "Oh, sorry . . . come in."

"What the hell's the matter with you?" asked Jorg.

"Sit down. I thought it was Lila . . ."

"You play peek-a-boo with Lila?"

"It's nothing."

"Serge, you've got to get rid of that girl, she's destroying your mind."

"She sharpens my pencils."

"Serge, she's too young for you."

"She's 30."

"And you're 60. That's 30 years."

"Thirty years is too much?"

"Of course."

"How about 20?" asked Serge, looking at Arlene.

"Twenty years is acceptable. Thirty years is obscene."

"Why don't you both get women your own age?" asked Arlene.

They both looked at her. "She likes to make little jokes," said Jorg. "Yes," said Serge, "she is funny. Come on, look, I'll show you what I'm doing . . ."

They followed him into the bedroom. He took off his shoes and lay flat on the bed. "See? Like this? All the comforts." Serge had his paint brushes on long handles and he painted on a canvas fastened to the ceiling. "It's my back. Can't paint ten minutes without stopping. This way I go on for hours."

"Who mixes your colors?"

"Lila. I tell her, 'Stick it in the blue. Now a bit of green.' She's quite good. Eventually I might even let her work the brushes, too, and I'll just lay around and read magazines."

Then they heard Lila coming up the stairway. She opened the door, came across the front room and entered the bedroom. "Hey," she said, "I see the old fuck's painting."

"Yeah," said Jorg, "he claims you hurt his back."

"I said no such thing."

"Let's go out and eat," said Arlene. Serge moaned and got up.

"Honest to Christ," said Lila. "He just lays around like a sick frog most of the time."

"I need a drink," said Serge. "I'll snap back."

They went down to the street together and moved toward The Sheep's Tick. Two young men in their mid-20's ran up. They had on turtleneck sweaters. "Hey, you guys are the painters, Jorg Swenson and Serge Maro!"

"Get the hell out of the way!" said Serge.

Jorg swung his ivory cane. He got the shorter of the young men right on the knee. "Shit," the young man said, "you've broken my leg!"

13

"I hope so," said Jorg. "Maybe you'll learn some damned civility!"

They moved on toward The Sheep's Tick. As they entered a buzzing arose from the diners. The headwaiter immediately rushed up, bowing and waving menus and speaking endearments in Italian, French and Russian.

"Look at that long, black hair in his nostrils," said Serge. "Truly sickening!"

"Yes," said Jorg, and then he shouted at the waiter, "HIDE YOUR NOSE!"

"Five bottles of your best wine!" screamed Serge, as they sat down at the best table.

The headwaiter vanished. "You two are real assholes," said Lila.

Jorg ran his hand up her leg. "Two living immortals are allowed certain indiscretions."

"Get your hand off my pussy, Jorg."

"It's not your pussy. It's Serge's pussy."

"Get your hand off Serge's pussy or I'll scream."

"My will is weak."

She screamed. Jorg removed his hand. The headwaiter came toward them with the wagon and bucket of chilled wine. He rolled it up, bowed and pulled one cork. He filled Jorg's glass. Jorg drained it. "It's shit, but O.K. Open the bottles!"

"All the bottles?"

"All the bottles, asshole, and be *quick* about it!"

"He's clumsy," said Serge. "Look at him. Shall we dine?"

"Dine?" said Arlene. "All you guys do is drink. I don't think I've seen either of you eat more than a soft-boiled egg."

"Get out of my sight, coward," Serge said to the waiter.

The headwaiter vanished.

"You guys shouldn't talk to people that way," said Lila.

"We've paid our dues," said Serge.

"You've got no right," said Arlene.

"I suppose not," said Jorg, "but it's interesting."

"People don't have to take that crap," said Lila.

"People accept what they accept," said Jorg. "They accept far worse."

"It's your paintings they want, that's all," said Arlene.

"*We* are our paintings," said Serge.

14

"Women are stupid," said Jorg.

"Be careful," said Serge. "They also are capable of terrible acts of vengeance . . ."

They sat for a couple of hours drinking the wine.

"Man is less delicate than the locust," said Jorg finally.

"Man is the sewer of the universe," said Serge.

"You guys are really assholes," said Lila.

"Sure are," said Arlene.

"Let's switch tonight," said Jorg. "I'll fuck your pussy and you fuck mine."

"Oh no," said Arlene, "none of that."

"Right," said Lila.

"I feel like painting now," said Jorg. "I'm bored with drinking."

"I feel like painting, too," said Serge.

"Let's get out of here," said Jorg.

"Listen," said Lila, "you guys haven't paid the bill yet."

"Bill?" screamed Serge. "You don't think we are going to pay money for this rotgut?"

"Let's go," said Jorg.

As they rose, the head waiter came up with the bill.

"This rotgut stinks," screamed Serge, jumping up and down. "I would never ask anyone to pay for stuff like this! I want you to know the proof is in the piss!"

Serge grabbed a half-full bottle of the wine, ripped open the waiter's shirt and poured the wine over his chest. Jorg held his ivory cane like a sword. The headwaiter looked confused. He was a beautiful young man with long fingernails and an expensive apartment. He was studying chemistry and had once won second prize in an opera competition. Jorg swung his cane and caught the waiter, hard, just below the left ear. The waiter turned very white and swayed. Jorg hit him three more times in the same spot and he dropped.

They walked out together, Serge, Jorg, Lila and Arlene. They were all drunk but there was a certain stature about them, something unique. They got out the door and went down the street.

A young couple seated at a table near the door had watched the entire proceedings. The young man looked intelligent, only a rather large mole near the end of his nose marred the effect. His girl was fat but lovable in a dark blue dress. She had once wanted to be a nun.

"Weren't they magnificent?" asked the young man.

"They were assholes," said the girl.

The young man waved for a third bottle of wine. It was going to be another difficult night.

SCREAM WHEN YOU BURN

Henry poured a drink and looked out the window at the hot and bare Hollywood street. Jesus Christ, it had been a long haul and he was still up against the wall. Death was next, death was always there. He'd made a dumb mistake and bought an underground newspaper and they were still idolizing Lenny Bruce. There was a photo of him, dead, right after the bad fix. All right, Lenny had been funny at times: "I can't come!"—that bit had been a masterpiece but Lenny really hadn't been all that good. Persecuted, all right, sure, physically and spiritually. Well, we all ended up dead, that was just mathematics. Nothing new. It was waiting around that was the problem. The phone rang. It was his girlfriend.

"Listen, you son of a bitch, I'm tired of your drinking. I had enough of that with my father . . ."

"Oh hell, it's not all that bad."

"It is, and I'm not going through it again."

"I tell you, you're making too much of it."

"No, I've had it, I tell you, I've had it. I saw you at the party, sending out for more whiskey, that's when I left. I've had it, I'm not going to take any more . . ."

She hung up. He walked over and poured a scotch and water. He walked into the bedroom with it, took off his shirt, pants, shoes, stockings. In his shorts he went to bed with the drink. It was 15 minutes to noon. No ambition, no talent, no chance. What kept him off the row was raw luck and luck never lasted. Well, it was too bad about Lu, but Lu wanted a winner. He emptied the glass and stretched out. He picked up Camus' *Resistance, Rebellion and*

17

Death . . . read some pages. Camus talked about anguish and terror and the miserable condition of Man but he talked about it in
such a comfortable and flowery way . . . his language . . . that one
got the feeling that things neither affected him *nor* his writing. In
other words, things might as well have been fine. Camus wrote
like a man who had just finished a large dinner of steak and french
fries, salad, and had topped it with a bottle of good French wine.
Humanity may have been suffering but not him. A wise man, perhaps, but Henry preferred somebody who screamed when they burned. He dropped the book to the floor and tried to sleep. Sleep was
always difficult. If he could sleep three hours in 24 he was satisfied.
Well, he thought, the walls are still here, give a man four walls and
he had a chance. Out on the streets, nothing could be done.

The doorbell rang. "Hank!" somebody screamed. "Hey, Hank!"

What the shit? he thought. Now what?

"Yeah?" he asked, lying there in his shorts.

"Hey! What are you doing?"

"Wait a minute . . ."

He got up, picked up his shirt and pants and walked into the
front room.

"What are you doing?"

"Getting dressed . . ."

"Getting dressed?"

"Yeah."

It was ten minutes after 12. He opened the door. It was the professor from Pasadena who taught English lit. He had a looker with
him. The prof introduced the looker. She was an editor in one of
the large New York publishing houses.

"Oh you sweet thing," he said, and walked up and squeezed her
right thigh. "I love you."

"You're fast," she said.

"Well, you know writers have always had to kiss the asses of
publishers."

"I thought it was the other way around."

"It isn't. It's the writer who's starving."

"She wants to see your novel."

"All I have is a hardcover. I can't give her a hardcover."

"Let her have one. They might buy it," said the prof.

They were talking about his novel, *Nightmare*. He figured she just wanted a free copy of the novel.

"We were going to Del Mar but Pat wanted to see you in the flesh."

"How nice."

"Hank read his poems to my class. We gave him $50. He was frightened and crying. I had to push him out in front of my class."

"I was indignant. Only $50. Auden used to get $2,000. I don't think he's that much better than I am. In fact . . ."

"Yes, we know what you think."

Henry gathered up the old Racing Forms from around the editor's feet.

"People owe me $1100. I can't collect. The sex mags have become impossible. I've gotten to know the girl in the front office. One Clara. 'Hello, Clara,' I phone her, 'did you have a nice breakfast?' 'Oh yes, Hank, did you?' 'Sure,' I tell her, 'two hard-boiled eggs.' 'I know what you're phoning about,' she answers. 'Sure,' I tell her, 'the same thing.' 'Well, we have it right here, our p.o. 984765 for $85.' 'And there's another one, Clara, your p.o. 973895 for five stories, $570.' 'Oh yes, well I'll try to get these signed by Mr. Masters.' 'Thank you, Clara,' I tell her. 'Oh that's all right,' she says, 'you fellows deserve your money.' 'Sure,' I say. And then she says, 'And if you don't get your money you'll phone again, won't you? Ha, ha, ha.' 'Yes, Clara,' I tell her, 'I'll phone again.'"

The professor and the editor laughed.

"I can't make it, god damn it, anybody want a drink?"

They didn't answer so Henry poured himself one. "I even tried to make it playing the horses. I started well but I hit a slump. I had to stop. I can only afford to win."

The professor started to explain his system for beating twenty-one at Vegas. Henry walked over to the editor.

"Let's go to bed," he said.

"You're funny," she said.

"Yeah," he said, "like Lenny Bruce. Almost. He's dead and I'm dying."

"You're still funny."

"Yeah, I'm the hero. The myth. I'm the unspoiled one, the one who hasn't sold out. My letters are auctioning for $250 back east. I can't buy a bag of farts."

"All you writers are always hollering 'wolf.'"

"Maybe the wolf has finally arrived. You can't live off your soul. You can't pay the rent with your soul. Try it some time."

"Maybe I ought to go to bed with you," she said.

"Come on, Pat," said the prof, standing up, "we've got to make Del Mar."

They walked to the door. "It was good to see you."

"Sure," Henry said.

"You'll make it."

"Sure," he said, "goodbye."

He walked back to the bedroom, took off his clothing and got back into bed. Maybe he could sleep. Sleep was something like death. Then he was asleep. He was at the track. The man at the window was giving him money and he was putting it into his wallet. It was a lot of money.

"You ought to get a new wallet," said the man, "that one's torn."

"No," he said, "I don't want people to know I'm rich."

The doorbell rang. "Hey Hank! Hank!"

"All right, all right . . . wait a minute . . ."

He put his clothes back on and opened the door. It was Harry Stobbs. Stobbs was another writer. He knew too many writers.

Stobbs walked in.

"You got any money, Stobbs?"

"Hell no."

"All right, I'll buy the beer. I thought you were rich."

"No, I was living with this gal in Malibu. She dressed me well, fed me. She booted me out. I'm living in a shower now."

"A shower?"

"Yes, it's nice. Real glass sliding doors."

"All right, let's go. You got a car?"

"No."

"We'll take mine."

They got into his '62 Comet and drove up toward Hollywood and Normandy.

"I sold an article to *Time*. Man, I thought I was in the big money. I got their check today. I haven't cashed it yet. Guess what it reads?" asked Stobbs.

"$800?"

"No, $165."

20

"What? *Time* magazine? 165 dollars?"

"That's right."

They parked and went in to a small liquor store for the beer. "My woman dumped me," Henry told Stobbs. "She claims I drink too much. A bareass lie." He reached into the cooler for two six-packs. "I'm tapering off. Bad party last night. Nothing but starving writers, and professors who were about to lose their jobs. Shop talk. Very wearing."

"Writers are whores," said Stobbs, "writers are the whores of the universe."

"The whores of the universe do much better, my friend."

They walked to the counter.

" 'Wings of Song,' " said the owner of the liquor store.

" 'Wings of Song,' " Henry answered.

The owner had read an article in the *L.A. Times* a year ago about Henry's poetry and had never forgotten. It was their Wings of Song routine. At first he had hated it, and now he found it amusing. Wings of Song, by god.

They got into the car and drove back. The mailman had been by. There was something in the box.

"Maybe it's a check," Henry said.

He took the letter inside, opened two beers and opened the letter. It said,

> "Dear Mr. Chinaski, I just finished reading your novel, *Nightmare*, and your book of poems, *Photographs From Hell*, and I think you're a great writer. I am a married woman, 52 years old, and my children are grown. I would very much like to hear from you. Respectfully, Doris Anderson."

The letter was from a small town in Maine.

"I didn't know that people still lived in Maine," he told Stobbs.

"I don't think they do," Stobbs said.

"They do. This one does."

Henry threw the letter in the trash sack. The beer was good. The nurses were coming home to the highrise apartment across the street. Many nurses lived there. Most of them wore see-through uniforms and the afternoon sun did the rest. He stood there with Stobbs watching them get out of their cars and walk through the glass entrance, to vanish to their showers and their tv sets and their closed doors.

"Look at that one," said Stobbs.

"Uh huh."

"There's another one."

"Oh my!"

We're acting like 15-year-olds, Henry thought. We don't deserve to live. I'll bet Camus never peeked out of windows.

"How are you going to make it, Stobbs?"

"Well, as long as I've got that shower, I've got it made."

"Why don't you get a job?"

"A job? Don't talk like a crazy man."

"I guess you're right."

"Look at that one! Look at the ass on that one!"

"Yes, indeed."

They sat down and worked at the beer.

"Mason," he told Stobbs, mentioning a young unpublished poet, "has gone to Mexico to live. He hunts meat with his bow and arrow, catches fish. He's got his wife and a servant girl. He's got four books out looking. Even wrote a Western. The problem is that when you're out of the country it's almost impossible to collect your money. The only way to collect your money is to threaten them with death. I'm good at those letters. But if you're a thousand miles away they know you'll cool off before you get to their door. I like hunting your own meat, though. It beats going to the A & P. You pretend those animals are editors and publishers. It's great."

Stobbs stayed around until 5 p.m. They bitched about writing, about how the top guys really stank. Guys like Mailer, guys like Capote. Then Stobbs left, and Henry took off his shirt, his pants, his shoes and stockings and went back to bed. The phone rang. It was on the floor near the bed. He reached down and picked it up. It was Lu.

"What are you doing? Writing?"

"I seldom write."

"Are you drinking?"

"Tapering off."

"I think you need a nurse."

"Let's go to the track tonight."

"All right. When will you be by?"

"6:30 O.K.?"

"6:30's O.K."

"Goodbye, then."

He stretched out in bed. Well, it was good to be back with Lu. She was good for him. She was right, he drank too much. If Lu drank like he did, he wouldn't want her. Be fair, man, be fair. Look what happened to Hemingway, always sitting with a drink in his hand. Look at Faulkner, look at them all. Well, shit.

The phone rang again. He picked it up.

"Chinaski?"

"Yeah?"

It was the poetess, Janessa Teel. She had a nice body but he'd never been to bed with her.

"I'd like you to come to dinner tomorrow night."

"I'm going steady with Lu," he said. God, he thought, I'm loyal. God, he thought, I'm a nice guy. God.

"Bring her with you."

"Do you think that would be wise?"

"It'll be all right with me."

"Listen, let me phone you tomorow. I'll let you know."

He hung up and stretched out again. For 30 years, he thought, I wanted to be a writer and now I'm a writer and what does it mean?

The phone rang again. It was Doug Eshlesham, the poet.

"Hank, baby . . ."

"Yeah, Doug?"

"I'm tapped, baby, I need a five, baby. Lemme have a fiver."

"Doug, the horses have smashed me. I'm flat, absolutely."

"Oh," said Doug.

"Sorry, baby."

"Well, all right."

Doug hung up. Doug owed him 15 right then. But he did have the fiver. He should have given Doug the fiver. Doug was probably eating dog food. I'm not a very nice guy, he thought. God, I'm not a very nice guy after all.

He stretched out in bed, full, in his unglory.

A COUPLE OF GIGOLOS

Being a gigolo is a very strange experience, especially if you're a non-professional gigolo. The house had two floors. Comstock lived with Lynne on the upper floor. I lived with Doreen on the lower floor. The house was in a beautiful setting at the foot of the Hollywood Hills. The ladies were both executives with high paying jobs. The house was stocked with good wine, good food, and one frazzle-assed dog. There was also a large black maid, Retha, who spent most of her time in the kitchen opening and closing the refrigerator door.

All the right magazines arrived at their appointed time each month, but Comstock and I didn't read them. We just lounged about, coming down off our hangovers, waiting for evening when the ladies would wine and dine us again on their expense accounts.

Comstock said Lynne was a very successful movie producer at a big studio. Comstock wore a beret, a silk scarf, a turquoise necklace, a beard, and he had a silken walk. I was a writer stalled on his second novel. I had my own quarters in a bombed-out apartment building in east Hollywood but I was seldom there.

My transportation was a '62 Comet. The young lady in the house across the way took great offense to my old car. I had to park in front of her house because it was one of the few level areas in the neighborhood and my car would not start on a grade. It hardly started on level ground and I'd sit out there pumping the pedal and hitting the starter and the smoke would billow out from under the car and the noise would be obnoxious and continuous. The lady would begin to scream as if she was going mad. It was one of the few times I was ashamed of being poor. I'd sit pumping and praying to get that '62 Comet started, and try to ignore the cries of rage from her expensive home. I'd pump and pump, the car would start, run a few feet, stall again.

"Get that stinking wreck away from in front of my house or I'll call the police!" Then the mad long screams. Finally she'd come out in a kimono, a young blonde, beautiful, but apparently completely crazy. She'd run up to the car door screaming and one of her breasts would fall out. She'd tuck it back in and the other breast would fall out. And then a leg would pop out of her slitted kimono. "Lady, please," I'd tell her, "I'm trying."

I'd finally get the car rolling and she'd stand in the center of the street with both breasts out screaming, *"Don't park your car here again, never, never, never!"* It was at times like this that I did consider looking for a job.

My lady, Doreen, needed me, however. She had trouble with the bag boy in the supermarket. I would go along and stand by her side and give her a sense of security. She couldn't confront him alone and always ended up throwing a handful of grapes in his face or reporting him to the manager or writing a six-page letter to the owner of the market. I could handle the bag boy for her. I even liked him, especially for the way he was able to snap open a large paper bag with one graceful flick of the wrist.

My first informal meeting with Comstock was interesting. We only had chatted over drinks with our ladies in the evening. One morning I was walking around the first floor in my shorts. Doreen had gone to work. I was thinking about getting dressed and going over to my place to check the mail. Retha, the maid, was used to me in my shorts. "Oh, man," she'd say, "your legs are so white. They're like chicken legs. Don't you ever get any sun?"

There was one kitchen and that was downstairs. I guess Comstock was hungry. We walked in at the same time. He wore an old white t-shirt with a wine stain on the front. I put on some coffee and Retha offered to fry us some bacon and eggs. Comstock sat down. "Well," I asked him, "how much longer do you think we can go on fooling them?"

"A long time. I need a rest."

"I think I'll hang in too."

"You bastards are really something," said Retha.

"Don't burn the eggs," said Comstock.

Retha served us our orange juice, toast, bacon and eggs. She sat down and ate with us, reading a copy of *Playgirl*.

"I'm just out of a real bad marriage," said Comstock. "I need a long, long rest."

"There's strawberry jam for your toast," said Retha. "Try some strawberry jam."

"Tell me about *your* marriage," I said to Retha.

"Well, I got me this lowdown no good lazy pool playin' . . ."

Retha told us all about him, finished her breakfast, and went upstairs and started vacuuming. Then Comstock told me about his marriage.

"Before our marriage it was fine. She showed me all her good cards but she had a half deck that she never let me see. I'd say more than a half deck." Comstock took a gulp of his coffee.

"Three days after the ceremony I came home and she had bought some miniskirts, the shortest miniskirts you ever saw. And when I came in she was sitting there shortening them. 'What are you doing?' I asked her, and she said, 'These fucking things are too long. I like to wear them without panties and I like to see men flash at my pussy when I slide off bar stools and stuff like that.'"

"She hit you with that card just like that?"

"Well, I might have had some warning. A couple of days before the marriage I took her over to meet my parents. She had on a conservative dress and my parents told her they liked it. She said, 'You like my dress, huh?' And she pulled her dress up and showed them her panties."

"You probably thought it was charming."

"In a way, yes. Anyhow, she started going around without panties in the miniskirts. They were so short that if she ducked her head you could see her bunghole."

"Did the boys like it?"

"I guess they did. When we'd walk into a place they'd look at her, then at me. They'd sit there thinking how can a guy go along with that?"

"Well, we all have our ways. What the hell. A pussy and a bunghole are only that. You can't make any more than that out of them."

"You might think that way until it happens to you. We'd leave a bar, get outside, and she'd say, 'Hey, did you see the bald guy in the corner? He really flashed on my pussy when I got up! I bet he goes home and beats off.' "

"Can I pour you another coffee?"

"Sure, and put in some scotch. You can call me Roger."

"Sure, Roger."

"I came home from work one evening and she was gone. She's broken every window and mirror in the place. She's written things like, 'Roger ain't shit!' 'Roger sucks assholes!' 'Roger drinks piss!' all over the walls. And she's gone. She's left a note. She's going to take a bus home to her mother in Texas. She's worried. Her mother has been in the madhouse ten times. Her mother needs her. That's what the note said."

"Another coffee, Roger?"

"Just the scotch. I went down to Greyhound and there she is in a miniskirt, flashing pussy, 18 guys circling around her with erections. I sat down next to her and she starts crying. 'A black guy,' she tells me, 'says I can make $1,000 a week if I do what he says. I ain't no whore, Roger!' "

Retha came back down the stairs, hit the refrigerator for some chocolate cake and ice cream, went into the bedroom, turned on the tv, lay down on the bed and started eating. She was a very heavy woman, but pleasant.

"Anyhow," said Roger, "I told her I loved her and we managed to get a refund on the ticket. I took her home. The next night a friend of mine comes over and she creeps up behind him and hits him over the head with a wooden salad spoon. No warning, no nothing. She just creeps up and whacks him. After he leaves she tells me that she'll be all right if I let her go to a ceramics class every Wednesday evening. All right, I say. But nothing works. She takes to attacking me with knives. There's blood everywhere. My blood. It's on the walls and in the rugs. She's very swift on her feet. She's into ballet, yoga, herbs, vitamins, eats seeds, nuts, all that shit, carries a bible in her purse, half the pages underlined in red ink. She shortens all her skirts another half inch. One night, I'm asleep and I wake up just in time. She's flying over the foot of the bed screaming, butcher knife in hand. I roll over and the knife plunges into the mattress five or six inches. I get up and knock her against the wall. She goes down and says, *You coward! You dirty coward, you hit a woman! You're yellow, yellow, yellow!'* "

"Well, I guess you shouldn't have hit her," I said.

"Anyhow, I moved out and began divorce proceedings but that wasn't the end of her. She kept following me. Once I was in the checkout line at a supermarket. She walked in and screamed at me, *'You dirty cocksucker! You fag!'* Another time she cornered me in a laundromat. I was taking my clothes out of the washer and putting them in the dryer. She just stood there and looked at me and didn't say anything. I left the clothes, got in my car and drove off. When I returned she wasn't there. I looked in the dryer and it was empty. She had taken my shirts, my shorts, my pants, my towels, my bedsheets, everything. I started getting letters in the mail written in red ink about her dreams. She dreamed all the time. And she'd cut out photographs from magazines and write all over them. I couldn't decipher the writing. I'd be sitting in my apartment at night and she'd walk by and throw gravel at my window and holler, *'Roger Comstock is a fairy.'* You could hear her for blocks."

"It all sounds very lively."

"Then I met Lynne and moved up here. I moved in the early morning. She doesn't know where I am. I quit my job. And here I am. I think I'll take Lynne's dog for a walk. She likes that. When she gets back from work I say, 'Hey, Lynne, I took your dog for a walk.' Then she smiles. She likes that."

"O.K.," I said.

"Hey, Boner!" Roger hollered. "Come on, Boner!" The idiot creature, soft of belly, salivated in. They left together.

I only lasted three more months. Doreen met some guy who could speak three languages and was an Egyptologist. I went back to my bombed-out court in east Hollywood.

I was coming out of my dentist's office in Glendale one day nearly a year later and there was Doreen getting into her car. I walked over and we went into a cafe and had coffee.

"How's the novel?" she asked.

"Still stalled," I said. "I don't think I'll ever finish the son of a bitch."

"You alone now?" she asked.

"No."

"I'm not alone either."

"Good."

"It's not good but it's all right."

"Is Roger still up there with Lynne?"

"She was going to dump him," Doreen told me. "Then he got drunk and fell off the balcony. He was paralyzed from the waist down. He collected $50,000 from the insurance company. Then he got better. Went from crutches to cane. He's able to walk Boner again. He recently took some marvelous photographs of Olvera Street. Listen, I've got to run. I'm going to London next week. A working vacation. All expenses paid! Goodbye."

"Goodbye."

Doreen jumped up, smiled, walked out, turned west and was gone. I lifted my coffeecup, took a sip, put it back down. The check lay on the table. $1.85. I had $2 which would just cover it plus the tip. How the hell I was going to pay my dentist was another matter.

THE GREAT POET

I went to see him. He was the great poet. He was the best narrative poet since Jeffers, still under 70 and famous throughout the world. Perhaps his two best-known books were *My Grief Is Better Than Your Grief, Ha!* and *The Dead Chew Gum in Languor.* He had taught at many universities, had won all the prizes, including the Nobel Prize. Bernard Stachman.

I climbed the steps of the YMCA. Mr. Stachman lived in Room 223. I knocked. "HELL, COME ON IN!" somebody screamed from inside. I opened the door and walked in. Bernard Stachman was in bed. The smell of vomit, wine, urine, shit and decaying food was in the air. I began to gag. I ran to the bathroom, vomited, then came out.

"Mr. Stachman," I said, "why don't you open a window?"

"That's a good idea. And don't give me any of that 'Mr. Stachman' shit, I'm Barney."

He was crippled, and after a great effort he managed to pull himself out of the bed and into the chair at his side. "Now for a good talk," he said. "I've been waiting for this."

At his elbow, on a table, was a gallon jug of dago red filled with cigarette ashes and dead moths. I looked away, then looked back. he had the jug to his mouth but most of the wine ran right back out, down his shirt, down his pants. Bernard Stachman put the jug back. "Just what I needed."

"You ought to use a glass," I said. "It's easier."

"Yes, I believe you're right." He looked around. There were a few dirty glasses and I wondered which one he would choose. He chose

31

the nearest one. The bottom of the glass was filled with a hardened yellow substance. It looked like the remains of chicken and noodles. He poured the wine. Then he lifted the glass and emptied it. "Yes, that's much better. I see you brought your camera. I guess you came to photograph me?"

"Yes," I said. I went over and opened the window and breathed in the fresh air. It had been raining for days and the air was fresh and clear.

"Listen," he said, "I been meaning to piss for hours. Bring me an empty bottle." There were many empty bottles. I brought him one. He didn't have a zipper, just buttons, with only the bottom button fastened because he was so bloated. He reached in and got his penis and rested the head on the lip of the bottle. The moment he began to urinate his penis stiffened and waved about, spraying piss all over—on his shirt, on his pants, in his face, and unbelievably, the last spurt went into his left ear.

"It's hell being crippled," he said.

"How did it happen?" I asked.

"How did what happen?"

"Being crippled."

"My wife. She ran me over with her car."

"How? Why?"

"She said she couldn't stand me anymore."

I didn't say anything. I took a couple of photos.

"I got photos of my wife. Want to see some photos of my wife?"

"All right."

"The photo album is there on top of the refrigerator."

I walked over and got it, sat down. There were just shots of high-heeled shoes and a woman's trim ankles, nylon-covered legs with garter belts, assorted legs in panty hose. On some of the pages were pasted ads from the meat market: chuck roast, 89¢ a pound. I closed the album. "When we divorced," he said, "she gave me these." Bernard reached under the pillow on his bed and pulled out a pair of high-heeled shoes with long spike heels. He'd had them bronzed. He stood them on the night table. Then he poured another drink. "I sleep with those shoes," he said, "I make love to those shoes and then wash them out."

I took some more photos.

"Here, you want a photo? Here's a good photo." He unbuttoned the lone button on his pants. He didn't have on any underwear. He took the heel of the shoe and wiggled it up his behind. "Here, take this one." I got the photo.

It was difficult for him to stand but he managed by holding onto the night table.

"Are you still writing, Barney?"

"Hell, I write all the time."

"Don't your fans interrupt your work?"

"Oh hell, sometimes the women find me but they don't stay long."

"Are your books selling?"

"I get royalty checks."

"What is your advice to young writers?"

"Drink, fuck and smoke plenty of cigarettes."

"What is your advice to older writers?"

"If you're still alive, you don't need any advice."

"What is the impulse that makes you create a poem?"

"What makes you take a shit?"

"What do you think of Reagan and unemployment?"

"I don't think of Reagan or unemployment. It all bores me. Like space flights and the Super Bowl."

"What are your concerns then?"

"Modern women."

"Modern women?"

"They don't know how to dress. Their shoes are dreadful."

"What do you think of Women's Liberation?"

"Any time they're willing to work the car washes, get behind the plow, chase down the two guys who just held up the liquor store, or clean up the sewers, anytime they're ready to get their tits shot off in the army, I'm ready to stay home and wash the dishes and get bored picking lint off the rug."

"But isn't there some logic in their demands?"

"Of course."

Stachman poured another drink. Even drinking from the glass, part of the wine dribbled down his chin and onto his shirt. He had the body odor of a man who hadn't bathed in months. "My wife," he said, "I'm still in love with my wife. Hand me that phone, will you?" I handed the phone to him. He dialed a number. "Claire? Hello, Claire?" He put the receiver down.

"What happened?" I asked.

"The usual. She hung up. Listen, let's get out of here, let's go to a bar. I've been in this damned room too long. I need to get out."

"But it's raining. It's been raining for a week. The streets are flooded."

"I don't care. I want to get out. She's probably fucking some guy right now. She's probably got her high heels on. I always made her leave her high heels on."

I helped Bernard Stachman get into an old brown overcoat. All the buttons were missing off the front. It was stiff with grime. It was hardly an L.A. overcoat, it was heavy and clumsy, it must have come from Chicago or Denver in the thirties.

Then we got his crutches and we climbed painfully down the YMCA stairway. Bernard had a fifth of muscatel in one of the pockets. We reached the entrance and Bernard assured me he could make it across the sidewalk and into the car. I was parked some distance from the curbing.

As I ran around to the other side to get in I heard a shout and then a splash. It was raining, and raining hard. I ran back around and Bernard had managed to fall and wedge himself in the gutter between the car and the curbing. The water swept around him, he was sitting up, the water rushed over him, ran down through his pants, lapped against his sides, the crutches floating sluggishly in his lap.

"It's all right," he said, "just drive on and leave me."

"Oh hell, Barney."

"I mean it. Drive on. Leave me. My wife doesn't love me."

"She's not your wife, Barney. You're divorced."

"Tell that to the Marines."

"Come on, Barney, I'm going to help you up."

"No, no. It's all right. I assure you. Just go ahead. Get drunk without me."

I picked him up, got the door open and lifted him into the front seat. He was very, very wet. Streams of water ran across the floorboards. Then I went around to the other side and got in. Barney unscrewed the cap off the bottle of muscatel, took a hit, passed the bottle to me. I took a hit. Then I started the car and drove, looking out through the windshield into the rain for a bar that we might possibly enter and not vomit the first time we got the look and smell of the urinal.

YOU KISSED LILLY

It was a Wednesday night. The television hadn't been much good.
Theodore was 56. His wife, Margaret, was 50. They had been married 20 years and had no children. Ted turned off the light. They
stretched out in the dark.

"Well," said Margy, "aren't you going to kiss me goodnight?"

Ted sighed and turned to her. He gave her a light kiss.

"You call that a kiss?"

Ted didn't answer.

"That woman on the program looked just like Lilly, didn't she?"

"I don't know."

"You know."

"Listen, don't start anything and there won't be anything."

"You just don't want to *discuss* things. You just want to clam
up. Be honest now. That woman on the progam looked like Lilly,
didn't she?"

"All right. There *was* a similarity."

"Did it make you think of Lilly?"

"Oh Christ . . ."

"Don't be evasive! Did it make you think of her?"

"For a moment or so, yes . . ."

"Did it make you feel good?"

"No, listen, Marge, that thing happened five years ago!"

"Does time change what happens?"

"I told you I was sorry."

"*Sorry!* Do you know what you *did* to me? Suppose I had done
that with some man? How would *you* feel?"

"I don't know. Do it and then I'll know."

"Oh, now you're being *flip!* It's a joke!"

"Marge, we've discussed this thing four or five hundred nights."

"When you were making love to Lilly did you kiss her like you kissed *me* tonight?"

"No, I guess not . . ."

"How then? How?"

"Jesus, stop it!"

"How?"

"Well, different."

"How was it different?"

"Well, there was a newness. I got excited . . ."

Marge sat up in bed and screamed. Then she stopped.

"And when you kiss me it's not exciting, is that it?"

"We're used to each other."

"But that's what *love* is: living and growing together."

"O.K."

" 'O.K.'? What do you mean—'O.K.'?"

"I mean, you're right."

"You don't say it like you mean it. You just don't want to talk. You've lived with me all these years. Do you know why?"

"I'm not sure. People just settle into things, like jobs. People just settle into things. It happens."

"You mean being with me is like a job? Is it like a job now?"

"You punch a time clock on a job."

"There you go again! This is a serious discussion!"

"All right."

" 'All right'? You loathsome ass! You're about to fall asleep!"

"Margy, what do you want me to do? That happened years ago!"

"All right, I'll tell you what I want you to do! I want you to kiss *me* like you did Lilly! I want you to *fuck* me like you did Lilly!"

"I can't do that . . ."

"Why? Because I don't excite you like Lilly did? Because I'm not *new?*"

"I hardly remember Lilly."

"You must remember *enough.* All right, you don't have to *fuck* me! Just *kiss* me like you did Lilly!"

"Oh my god, Margy, *please* let off, I beg you!"

"I want to know *why* we've lived all these years together! Have I wasted my life?"

36

"Everybody does, almost everybody does."

"Waste their lives?"

"I think so."

"If you could only *guess* how much I hate you!"

"Do you want a divorce?"

"Do I want a divorce? Oh my god, how *calm* you are! You ruin my whole god damned life and then ask me if I want a divorce! I'm 50 years old! I've given you my life! Where do I go from here?"

"You can go to hell! I'm tired of your voice. I'm tired of your bitching."

"Suppose I had done that with a man?"

"I wish you had. I wish you would!"

Theodore closed his eyes. Margaret sobbed. Outside a dog barked. Somebody tried to start a car. It wouldn't start. It was 65 degrees in a small town in Illinois. James Carter was president of the United States.

Theodore began to snore. Margaret went to the bottom drawer of the dresser and got the gun out. A .22 revolver. It was loaded. She got back into bed with her husband.

Margaret shook him. "Ted, darling, you're *snoring* . . ."

She shook him again.

"What is it . . . ?" Ted asked.

She took the safety off the gun and put the gun to the part of his chest nearest her and pulled the trigger. The bed jolted and she pulled the gun away. A sound much like a fart came out of Theodore's mouth. He didn't seem to be in pain. The moon shone through the window. She looked and the hole was small and there wasn't much blood. Margaret moved the gun to the other side of Theodore's chest. She pulled the trigger again. This time he made no sound at all. But he continued to breathe. She watched him. The blood was coming. The blood stank terribly.

Now that he was dying she almost loved him. But Lilly, when she thought about Lilly . . . Ted's mouth on hers, and all the rest, then she wanted to shoot him again . . . Ted had always looked good in a turtleneck and he looked good in green, and when he farted in bed he always first turned away—he never farted against her. He seldom missed a day at work. He'd miss tomorrow . . .

Margaret sobbed for a while and then went to sleep.

★ ★ ★

When Theodore awakened he felt as if there were long sharp reeds stuck into each side of his chest. He felt no pain. He put his hands on his chest and then lifted them in the moonlight. His hands were covered with blood. It confused him. He looked at Margaret. She was asleep and in her hand was the gun he had taught her to use for her own protection.

He sat up and the blood began exiting more quickly from the two holes in his chest. Margaret had shot him while he had been asleep. For fucking Lilly. He hadn't even been able to climax with Lilly.

He thought, I'm almost dead but if I can get away from her I might have a chance.

Theodore gently reached over and unclasped Margaret's fingers from the gun. The safety catch was still off.

I don't want to kill you, he thought, I just want to get away. I think I've wanted to get away for at least 15 years.

He managed to get out of bed. He took the gun and pointed it at Margaret's upper thigh, right leg. He fired.

Margy screamed and he put his hand over her mouth. He waited some minutes and then took his hand away.

"What are you *doing*, Theodore?"

He pointed the gun at Margaret's upper thigh, left leg. He fired. He stopped her new scream by putting his hand over her mouth again. He held it there some minutes, then took it away.

"You kissed Lilly," Margaret said.

There were two bullets left in the gun. Ted straightened and looked at the holes in his chest. The hole on the right side had stopped bleeding. The hole on the left side spurted a thin needle-like line of red at regular intervals.

"I'll *kill* you!" Margy told him from the bed.

"You *really* want to, don't you?"

"Yes, *yes*! And I *will*!"

Ted began to feel dizzy and sick. Where were the cops? Surely they had heard all the gunshots? Where *were* they? Couldn't anybody hear gunfire?

He saw the window. He fired at the window. He was getting weaker. He fell to his knees. He moved on his knees toward another window. He fired again. The bullet made a round hole in the glass but it didn't shatter. A black shadow passed in front of him. Then it was gone.

He thought, I've got to get this gun out of here!

Theodore gathered the last of his strength. He threw the gun against the window pane. The glass broke but the gun fell back inside of the house . . .

As he became conscious his wife was standing over him. She was actually *standing* on the two legs he had shot. She was reloading the gun.

"I'm going to kill you," she said.

"Margy, for Christ's sake, listen! I *love* you!"

"*Crawl*, you lying dog!"

"Margy, please. . . ."

Theodore began to crawl toward another bedroom.

She followed him. "So, it *excited* you to kiss Lilly?"

"No, no! I didn't like it! I hated it!"

"I'll blow those damned kissing lips right off your mouth!"

"Margy, my god!"

She put the gun to his mouth.

"Here's a *kiss* for you!"

She fired. The bullet blew away part of his lower lip and part of his jaw bone. He remained conscious. He saw one of his shoes on the floor. He gathered his strength again and threw the shoe at another window. The glass broke and the shoe fell outside.

Margaret took the gun and pointed it to her breast. She pulled the trigger . . .

When the police broke down the door Margaret was standing and holding the gun.

"All right, madam, drop the gun!" said one of the cops.

Theodore was still trying to crawl away. Margaret aimed the gun at him, fired and missed. Then she dropped to the floor in her purple nightgown.

"What the hell happened?" one of the cops asked, bending over Theodore.

Theodore turned his head. His mouth was a blob of red.

"Skirrr," said Theodore, "skirrr . . ."

"I hate these domestic quarrels," the other cop said. "Real messy . . ."

"Yeah," said the first cop.

"I had a fight with my wife just this morning. You can never tell."
"Skirrr," said Theodore . . .

Lilly was at home looking at an old Marlon Brando movie on television. She was alone. She'd always been in love with Marlon.
She farted gently. She lifted her robe and began to play with herself.

HOT LADY

Monk walked in. It seemed very dusty in there and dimmer than in the usual places. He walked toward the far end of the bar and sat down next to a big blonde who was smoking a cigarillo and drinking a Hamm's. She farted as Monk sat down. "Good evening," he said, "my name's Monk." "My name's Mud," she said, which immediately dated her.

As Monk sat there a skeleton rose from behind the bar where it had been sitting on a stool. The skeleton walked over to Monk. Monk ordered a scotch on the rocks and the skeleton reached out with its hands and began to make the drink. It spilled a goodly bit of scotch on the bar but it did manage the drink and it did pick up Monk's money, put it in the register and bring back the correct change.

"What's the matter?" Monk asked the lady, "can't they afford union help around here?"

"Ah fuck," said the lady, "that's Billy's trick. Can't you see the fucking wires? He operates that thing with wires. He thinks it's very funny."

"This place is strange," said Monk. "It stinks of death."

"Death doesn't stink," said the lady, "only the living stink, only the dying stink, only the decaying stink. Death doesn't stink."

A spider dropped down on an invisible thread between them and slowly spun around. It was golden in the dim light. Then it ran back up its thread and was gone.

"First spider I ever saw in a bar," said Monk.

"It lives on bar flies," said the lady.

"Christ, this place is full of bad jokes."

The lady farted. "A kiss for you," she said.

"Thank you," said Monk.

A drunk at the other end of the bar put some money in the juke-box and the skeleton came out from behind the bar and walked up to the lady and bowed. The lady got up and danced with the skeleton. They danced around and around. The only people that could be seen in the bar were the lady, the skeleton, the drunk and Monk. It was a slow night. Monk lit a Pall Mall and worked on his drink. The piece ended and the skeleton went back behind the bar and the lady came back and sat down beside Monk.

"I remember," said the lady, "when all the celebrities came in here. Bing Crosby, Amos and Andy, the Three Stooges. This place really used to swing."

"I like it better this way," said Monk.

The jukebox started again. "Care to dance?" asked the lady.

"Why not?" said Monk.

They got up and began dancing. The lady wore lavender and smelled of lilacs. But she was quite fat and her skin was orange in color and her false teeth seemed to chew quietly on a dead mouse.

"This place reminds me of Herbert Hoover," said Monk.

"Hoover was a great man," said the lady.

"Like hell," said Monk. "If Franky D. hadn't come along we all would have starved to death.

"Franky D. got us into the war," said the lady.

"Well," said Monk, "he had to protect us from the fascist hordes."

"Don't tell me about the fascist hordes," said the lady. "My brother died fighting Franco in Spain."

"Abraham Lincoln Brigade?" asked Monk.

"Abraham Lincoln Brigade," said the lady.

They were dancing very close and the lady suddenly stuck her tongue into Monk's mouth. He pushed it back out with his tongue. She tasted like old postage stamps and the dead mouse. The song ended. They walked over and sat down.

The skeleton walked over to them. It had a vodka and orange in one hand. It stood in front of Monk and threw the vodka and orange into his face, then walked off.

"What's wrong with him?" asked Monk.

"It's very jealous," said the lady. "It saw me kiss you."

"You call that a kiss?"

"I've kissed some of the greatest men of all time."

"I imagine you have—like Napoleon, Henry VIII and Caesar."

The lady farted. "A kiss for you," she said.

"Thank you," said Monk.

"I guess I am getting old," said the lady. "You know we talk about prejudices but we never talk about the prejudice everyone has against the old."

"Yeah," said Monk.

"I'm not *really* old, though," said the lady.

"No," said Monk.

"I still get monthlies," said the lady.

Monk waved the skeleton over for two more drinks. The lady switched to scotch on the rocks. They both had scotch on rocks. The skeleton walked back and sat down.

"You know," said the lady, "I was there when the Babe had two strikes on him and he pointed to the wall and on the next pitch he hit the ball right over the wall."

"I thought that was a myth," said Monk.

"Myth, shit," said the lady, "I was there. I saw it happen."

"You know," said Monk, "that's wonderful. You know it's exceptional people who make the world go round. They kind of work the miracles for us, while we sit around on our fannies."

"Yeah," said the lady.

They sat and nipped at their drinks. Outside you could hear the traffic going up and down Hollywood Boulevard. The sound was persistent, like the tide, like waves, almost like an ocean, and it was an ocean: there were sharks out there and barracuda and jellyfish and octopi and suckerfish and whales and mollusks and sponges and grunion and the like. Inside, it was more like a separate fishtank.

"I was there," said the lady, "when Dempsey almost murdered Willard. Jack was just off the boxcars and mean as a starved tiger. You never saw anything like it before or since."

"You say you still have monthlies?"

"That's right," said the lady.

"They say Dempsey had cement or plaster in his gloves, they say he soaked them in water and let them harden, that's why he busted up Willard like he did," said Monk.

"That's a fucking untruth," said the lady. "I was there, I saw those gloves."

"I think you're crazy," said Monk.

"They thought Joan of Arc was crazy too," said the lady.

"I suppose you saw Joan of Arc get burned," said Monk.

"I was there," said the lady. "I saw it."

"Bullshit."

"She burned. I saw her burn. It was so horrible and beautiful."

"What was beautiful about it?"

"The way she burned. It started at her feet. It was like a nest of red snakes and they crawled up her legs and then it was like a blazing red curtain and she had her face turned up and you could smell the flesh burning and she was still alive but she never screamed. Her lips were moving and she was praying but she never screamed."

"Bullshit," said Monk, "anybody would scream."

"No," said the lady, "not anybody would scream. People are different."

"Flesh is flesh, and pain is pain," said Monk.

"You underestimate the human spirit," said the lady.

"Yeah," said Monk.

The lady opened her purse. "Here, I wanna show you something." She took out a matchbook, struck a match and held the palm of her left hand out. She held the match underneath her palm and let it burn until the match went out. There was the sweet smell of burnt flesh.

"That's pretty good," said Monk, "but it's not the entire body."

"It doesn't matter," said the lady. "The principle's the same."

"No," said Monk, "it's not the same thing."

"Balls," said the lady. She stood up and put a match to the hem of her lavender dress. The material was thin and gauze-like and the flames began to lick around her legs and then began to crawl up toward her waist.

"Jesus Christ," said Monk. "What the hell are you doing?"

"Proving a principle," said the lady.

The flames rose higher. Monk leaped off his stool and tackled the lady. He rolled her over and over on the floor and beat at her dress with his hands. Then the fire was out. The lady got back on her barstool and sat there. Monk sat down beside her, shaking. The bartender walked up. He was dressed in a clean white shirt, black vest, bow tie, striped blue and white pants.

"I'm sorry, Maude," he said to the lady, "but you gotta go. You've had enough for tonight."

"O.K., Billy," said the lady, and she finished her drink, got up and walked out the door. Before she did she said goodnight to the drunk at the other end of the bar.

"My god," said Monk, "she's too god damned much."

"Did she pull her Joan of Arc act again?" asked the bartender.

"Hell, you saw it, didn't you?"

"No, I was talking to Louie," he pointed to the drunk at the end of the bar.

"I thought you were upstairs working those wires."

"What wires?"

"The wires on the skeleton."

"What skeleton?" asked the bartender.

"Now come on," said Monk, "don't give me any shit."

"What are you talking about?"

"There was a skeleton in here serving drinks. He even danced with Maude."

"I've been here all night, stranger," said the bartender.

"I said, 'Don't give me any shit!'"

"I'm not giving you any shit," said the bartender. He turned to the drunk at the end of the bar. "Hey, Louie, you seen a skeleton in here?"

"A skeleton?" asked Louie. "What are you talking about?"

"You tell this man that I've been right here behind the bar all night," said the bartender.

"Billy's been here all night, stranger. And neither of us has seen a skeleton."

"Give me another scotch on the rocks," said Monk. "Then I've got to get out of here."

The bartender brought the scotch on rocks. Monk drank it and then he got out of there.

IT'S A DIRTY WORLD

I drove along Sunset, late one evening, stopped for a signal, and at a bus stop saw this dyed redhead with a brutal and ravaged face, powdered, painted, that said "this is what life does to us." I could imagine her drunk, screaming across the room at some man and I was glad the man wasn't me. She saw me looking at her and waved, "Hey, how about a ride?" "O.K.," I said, and she ran across two lanes of traffic to get in. We drove along and she showed me a bit of leg. Not too bad. I drove not saying anything. "I want to go to Alvarado Street," she said. I figured as much. That's where they hung out. From Eighth and Alvarado on up, the bars across the park and around the corners, all the way up to where the hill began. I'd sat in those bars for quite a few years and knew the action. Most of the girls just wanted a drink and a place to stay. In those dark bars they didn't look too bad. We approached Alvarado. "Can I have 50 cents?" she asked. I reached in and got two quarters. "I ought to be able to cop a feel for that." She laughed. "Go ahead." I pulled her dress back and pinched her gently right where the stocking ended. I almost said, "Shit, let's get a fifth and go to my place." I could see myself stabbing that thin body, I could almost hear the springs. Then I could see her later sitting in a chair, cursing and talking and laughing. I passed. She got out at Alvarado and I watched her walking across the street, trying to shake it like she had something. I drove on. I owed the state $606 income tax. I'd have to skip a piece of ass now and then.

I parked outside the Chinaman's and went in and got a bowl of chicken won ton. The guy sitting to my right had his left ear missing. There was just a hole in his head, a dirty hole with a lot of hair around it. No ear at all. I looked into the hole and then went back to the chicken won ton. It didn't taste as good. Then another guy came in and sat on my left. He was a bum. He ordered a cup of coffee. He looked at me, "Hello, Wino," he said.

"Hello," I answered.

"Everybody calls *me* 'Wino,' so I thought I'd call you one."

"That's all right. I used to be one."

He stirred his coffee. "Those little bubbles on top of the coffee. There. Mother used to say that meant money was coming my way. It didn't work out that way."

Mother? This man once had a mother?

I finished my bowl and left them there, the guy without an ear and the bum looking at the bubbles in his coffee.

This is turning out to be a hell of a night, I thought. Guess not much more can happen. I was wrong.

I decided to walk across Alameda to buy some stamps. The traffic was heavy and they had a young cop directing traffic. There was some action going on. A young man in front of me kept hollering at the cop. "Come on, let us across, what the hell! We've been standing here long enough!" The cop kept waving the traffic through. "Come on, what the hell's wrong with you?" the kid yelled. This kid's gotta be nuts, I thought. He was nice looking, young, big, around six-three, two hundred pounds. White t-shirt. Nose a little too big. He might have had a few beers but he wasn't drunk. Then the cop blew his whistle and motioned for the crowd to cross. The kid stepped into the street. "All right, come on everybody, it's *safe* now, it's *safe* to cross!" That's what you think, kid, was my thought. The kid was waving his arms. "Come on, everybody!" I was walking right behind him. I saw the cop's face. It got very white. I saw the eyes narrow to slits. He was a short, heavyset, young cop. He moved toward the kid. Oh jesus, here it comes. The kid saw the cop moving toward him. "Don't you TOUCH me! Don't you dare TOUCH me!" The cop grabbed him by the right arm, said something to him, tried to guide the kid back to the curbing. The kid broke the grip and walked off. The cop ran up behind him, got a hammerlock on the kid. The kid broke out of that and then they were scuffling, whirling around. You could hear their feet in the street. People stood and watched from a distance. I was right on top of them. Several times I had to step back as they scuffled. I didn't have any

48

god damned sense either. Then they were up on the sidewalk. The cop's hat flew off. That's when I got a bit jumpy. The cop didn't look much like a cop without his cap, but he still had his club and his gun. The kid broke away again and started to run off. The cop leaped on him from behind, got an arm around his neck and tried to pull him over backwards, but the kid just stood there. And then he broke free. Finally the cop had him pinned against an iron guardrail outside a Standard Station parking lot. A white kid and a white cop. I looked across the street and saw five young blacks grinning and watching. They were lined up against a wall. The cop had his cap back on and was leading the kid down the street to a call box.

I went in and got my stamps out of the machine. It was a screwy night. I almost expected a snake to drop out of there. But I just got stamps. I looked up and saw my friend Benny. "Did you catch the action, Benny?"

"Yeah, when they get him to the station they'll put on leather gloves and beat hell out of him."

"You think so?"

"Sure. The city's just like the county. They beat hell out of them. I just got out of the new county jail. They let the new cops work out on the prisoners there to get experience. You could hear them screaming as the cops beat them. They brag about it. While I was in, one cop walked past and said, 'I just beat hell out of a wino!'"

"I've heard about it."

"They allow you one phone call and this guy was on the phone too long and they kept telling him to get off. He kept saying, 'just a minute, just a minute!' and finally one cop got pissed and hung the phone up and the guy screamed, 'I've got my rights, you can't do that!'"

"What happened?"

"About four cops grabbed the guy. They took him so fast that his feet didn't even touch the ground. They took him in the next room. You could hear him, they worked him over good. You know, they had us there, bending over, looking up our asses, looking in our shoes for dope, and they brought the kid out naked and he was bent over and trembling, shivering. You could see red welts all over his body. They just left him there, trembling against that wall. He had really had it."

"Yeah," I said, "I was driving past the Union Rescue Mission one night and two cops in a squad car were picking up a drunk. A cop got in the back seat with the drunk and I heard the drunk say 'you dirty motherfucking cop!' and I saw the cop take his club and jam the end of it, hard, right into the guy's stomach. It was a hell of a blow and made me a little sick. It could have broken the stomach open or caused internal bleeding."

"Yeah, it's a dirty world."

"You said it, Benny. See you around. Watch yourself."

"Sure. You too."

I found the car and drove on back up Sunset. When I got to Alvarado I turned south and drove down nearly to Eighth Street. I parked, got out, found a liquor store and bought a fifth of whiskey. Then I walked into the nearest bar. There she was. My redhead with the brutal face. I walked up, patted the fifth. "Let's go." She finished the drink and walked out behind me. "Nice evening," she said. "Oh, yeah," I answered.

When we got to my place she went to the bathroom and I rinsed out two glasses. There's no way out, I thought, there's no way out of anything.

She came into the kitchen, put herself up against me. She had put on fresh lipstick. She kissed me, working her tongue around in my mouth. I lifted her dress and got a handful of panty. We stood under the electric light, locked. Well, the state would have to wait a little longer for their income tax. Maybe Governor Deukmejian would understand. We broke, I poured two drinks and we walked into the other room.

900 POUNDS

Eric Knowles awakened in the motel room and looked around. There were Louie and Gloria wrapped around each other on the other half of the king-size bed. Eric found a warm bottle of beer, opened it, took it into the bathroom and drank it while under the shower. He was damned sick. He'd heard about the warm beer theory from experts. It didn't work. He stepped out of the shower and vomited into the toilet. Then he stepped back into the shower. That was the trouble with being a writer, that was the main trouble—leisure time, excessive leisure time. You had to wait around for the buildup until you could write and while you were waiting you went crazy, and while you were going crazy you drank and the more you drank the crazier you got. There was nothing glorious about the life of a writer or the life of a drinker. Eric toweled off, got into his shorts and walked into the other room. Louie and Gloria were awakening.

"Oh, shit," said Louie, "my god."

Louie was another writer. He didn't pay the rent with it like Eric did, Gloria paid Louie's rent. Three-fourths of the writers Eric knew in Los Angeles and Hollywood were supported by women; those writers were not as talented with the typewriter as they were with their women. They sold themselves to their women spiritually and physically.

He heard Louie in the bathroom vomiting and hearing it started Eric going again. He found an empty paper bag and each time Louie heaved Eric heaved. It was some close harmony.

Gloria was rather nice. She had just hooked on as an assistant professor at a northern California college. She stretched out on the bed and said, "You guys are something else. The vomit twins."

Louie stepped out of the bathroom. "Hey, are you makng fun of me?"

"No way, kiddo. It was just a hard night for me."

"It was a hard night for all of us."

"I think I'll try the warm beer cure again," said Eric. He twisted the top off a bottle and tried it again.

"That was something, the way you subdued her," said Louie.

"What do you mean?"

"I mean, when she came at you over the top of the coffee table, you did it all in slow motion. You weren't excited at all. You just got her by one of her arms, then the other, and rolled her over. Then you got on top of her and said, 'What the hell's the matter with you?' "

"This beer is working," said Eric. "You ought to try it."

Louie twisted the top off a bottle and sat down on the edge of the bed. Louie edited a little magazine, *Riot of the Rats*. It was a mimeo. As a little magazine it was no better or worse than the rest of them. They all got very tiresome; the talent was thin and inconsistent. Louie was now on his 15th or 16th issue.

"It was her house," said Louie, thinking about the night before. "She said it was her house and for us all to get out of there."

"Diverging viewpoints and ideals. They always cause trouble and there are always diverging viewpoints and ideals. Besides, it *was* her house," said Eric.

"I think I'll try one of those beers," said Gloria. She got up and got into her dress and found a warm beer. Nice looking professor, thought Eric.

They sat there trying to force the beers down.

"Anybody for television?" asked Louie.

"Don't you dare," said Gloria.

Suddenly there was an enormous explosion, it shook the walls.

"Jesus!" said Eric.

"What was that?" asked Gloria.

Louie walked to the door and opened it. They were on the second floor. There was a balcony and the motel was built around a swimming pool. Louie looked down. "You're not going to believe this but there's a five hundred pound guy down there in the swimming pool. That explosion you heard was when he jumped into the water. I never saw a guy so big. He's enormous. And he's got someone with him, weighs about four hundred pounds. Looks like his son. Now the son is going to jump in. Hold on!"

There was another explosion. The walls shook again. Fountains of water leaped out of the pool.

"Now they're swimming side by side. What a sight!"

Eric and Gloria walked to the door and looked out.

"This is a dangerous situation," said Eric.

"What do you mean?"

"I mean, looking down at all that fat we're apt to holler something at them. All very childish, you know. But hungover like this anything can happen."

"Yeah, I can just see them running up here and pounding on the door," said Louie. "How are we going to handle nine hundred pounds?"

"No way, even in good health."

"In bad health, no chance at all."

"Right."

"HEY FAT BOY!" Louie yelled down.

"Oh, no," said Eric, "oh no, please. I'm sick . . ."

Both of the fat men looked up from the swimming pool. They were both wearing light blue trunks.

"*Hey, fat boy!*" yelled Louie. "*I bet if you farted, you'd blow seaweed from here to Bermuda!*"

"Louie," said Eric, "there's no seaweed down there."

"*There's no seaweed down there, fat boy!*" yelled Louie. "*You must have sucked it up your ass!*"

"Oh, my god," said Eric, "I'm a writer because I'm a coward and now I face sudden and violent death."

The biggest fat man climbed out of the pool and the smaller one followed him. They could hear them coming up the stairway, plop, plop, plop. The walls shook.

Louie shut the door and hooked the chain.

"What has any of this got to do with a decent and abiding literature?" asked Eric.

"Nothing, I guess," answered Louie.

"You and your fucking little mimeo machine," said Eric.

"I'm scared," said Gloria.

"We're all scared," said Louie.

Then they were at the door. BAM, BAM, BAM, BAM!

"Yeah?" answered Louie. "What is it?"

"Open the fucking door!"

"There's nobody in here," said Eric.

"I'll teach you bastards!"

"Oh, please *do* teach me, sir!" said Eric.

"Now what did you say that for?" asked Gloria.

"Damn," said Eric, "I'm just trying to agree with him."

"Open up or I'm coming through!"

"We might as well make you work for it," said Louie. "Let's see what you can do."

They heard the sound of flesh straining against the door. They could see the door bend and give.

"You and your fucking mimeo machine," said Eric.

"It was a good machine."

"Help me brace this door," said Eric.

They stood bracing the door against the massive weight. The door weakened. Then they heard another voice. *"Hey, what the hell's going on up there?"*

"I'm going to teach these punks a lesson, that's what's going on!"

"You break that door and I'm going to call the police!"

"What?"

There was one more lunge, then it was quiet. Except for the voices.

"I'm on parole for assault and battery. Maybe I better go easy here."

"Yeah, cool off, you don't want to hurt nobody."

"But they spoiled my swim."

"There are things more important than swimming, man."

"Yeah, like eating," said Louie through the door.

BAM! BAM! BAM! BAM!

"What do you want?" asked Eric.

"Listen you guys! If I hear one more sound out of you, just one sound, I'm coming in!"

Eric and Louie were silent. They could hear the two fat men going down the stairway.

"I think we could have taken them," said Eric. "Fat guys can't move. They're easy."

"Yeah," said Louie, "I think we could have taken them. I mean, if we had really wanted to."

"We're out of beer," said Gloria, "I sure could use a cold beer. My nerves are completely shot."

"O.K., Louie," said Eric, "you go out and get the beers, I'll pay for them."

"No," said Louie, "you go get them. I'll pay."

"I'll pay," said Eric, "and we'll send Gloria."

"O.K." said Louie.

Eric gave Gloria the money and the instructions and they opened the door and let her out. The swimming pool was empty. It was a nice California morning, smoggy, stale and listless.

"You and your fucking mimeo machine," said Eric.

"It's a good magazine," said Louie, "it's as good as most."

"I suppose you're right."

Then they stood and sat and sat and stood waiting for Gloria to get back with the cold beer.

DECLINE AND FALL

It was a Monday afternoon in The Hungry Diamond. There were only two people in there, Mel and the bartender. Monday afternoon in Los Angeles is nowhere — even Friday night is nowhere — but especially Monday afternoon. The bartender, whose name was Carl, was drinking from under the bar and standing near Mel, who was humped leisurely over a stale green beer. "I gotta tell you something," said Mel. "Go ahead," said the bartender.

"Well, I got this phone call the other night from a guy I used to work with in Akron. He lost his job drinking and he married a nurse and this nurse supports him. I don't have much feeling for these people — but you know how people are, they kind of hang on to you."

"Yeah," said the bartender.

"Anyhow, they phone me — listen, give me another beer, this shit tastes awful."

"Okay, just drink it a little faster; it begins to lose body after an hour."

"All right . . . They tell me they've solved the meat shortage — I think 'What meat shortage?' — and to come on over. I've got nothing to do so I go over. The Rams are playing and this guy, Al, he turns on the tv and we watch. Erica, her name is, she's in the kitchen mixing a salad and I've brought a couple of six-packs. I say hello, Al opens a few bottles, it's nice and warm in there, the oven's on.

"Well, it's comfortable. They look like they haven't had an argument in a couple of days and the state of affairs is calm. Al says something about Reagan and something about unemployment but

57

I can't respond; it all bores me. You see, I don't give a damn if the country is rotten or not, so long as *I* make it."

"Right," said the bartender, taking a drink from under the bar.

"All right. She comes out and sits and drinks her beer. Erica. The nurse. She says that all the doctors treat their patients like cattle. She says that all the damned doctors are on the make. They think their own shit doesn't stink. She'd rather have Al than any doctor alive. Now that's a silly statement, isn't it?"

"I never met Al," said the barkeep.

"So we're playing cards and the Rams are losing and after a few hands Al says to me, 'You know, I got a strange wife. She likes to have somebody watch while we do the thing.' 'That's right,' she says, 'that's what really stimulates me.' And Al says, 'But it's so hard to get somebody to watch. You'd think it would be easy to get somebody to watch, but it's hard as hell.'

"I don't say anything. I ask for two cards and raise a nickel. She lays down her cards and Al lays down his cards and they both stand up. She starts to move back across the room and Al follows her. 'You whore,' he says, 'you god-damned whore!' Here's this guy calling his wife a whore. 'You whore!' he screams. He corners her in one corner of the room and slaps her, rips her blouse off. 'You whore!' he screams again, and slaps her and knocks her down. Her skirt is torn and she kicks her legs and screams.

"He picks her up and kisses her, then throws her on the couch. He's all over her, kissing her and ripping at her clothes. Then he's got her panties off and he's at work. While he's doing this she's looking out from underneath to see if I'm watching. She sees that I'm watching and she starts squirming like a mad snake. They really go to it, finish it off; she gets up and goes to the bathroom and Al goes into the kitchen for more beers. 'Thanks,' he says when he comes out, 'you were a big help.' "

"Then what happened?" asked the barkeep.

"Well, then the Rams finally scored, and there was a lot of noise on the tv, and she comes out of the bathroom and goes into the kitchen.

"Al starts in on Reagan again. He says it is the beginning of the Decline and Fall of the West, just like Spengler said. Everybody is so greedy and decadent, the decay has really set in. He goes along that line for some time.

"Then Erica calls us into the breakfast nook where the table is all set and we sit down. It smells good—a roast. There are slices of pineapple on top of it. It looks like an upper shank; I can see what almost looks like a knee. 'Al,' I say, 'that thing really looks like a human leg from the knee up.' 'That,' says Al, 'is exactly what it is.'"

"He said that?" asked the barkeep, taking a drink from under the bar.

"Yeah," answered Mel, "and when you hear something like that you don't know exactly what to think. What would *you* think?"

"I'd think," said the barkeep, "that he was joking."

"Of course. So I said, 'Great, cut me a nice slice.' And Al did. There was mashed potatoes and gravy, corn, heated bread and the salad. There were stuffed olives in the salad. Al said, 'Try a little of that hot mustard on that meat, it goes good.' So I put some on. The meat wasn't bad.

" 'Listen Al,' I said, 'this isn't really bad. What is it?' 'It's like I told you, Mel,' he answers, 'it's a human leg, the upper flank. It's a 14-year-old boy we found hitchhiking on Hollywood Boulevard. We took him in and fed him and he watched Erica and me do the thing for three or four days and then we got tired of doing that, so we slaughtered him, cleaned out the innards, ran that down the garbage disposal and dropped him into the freezer. It's a hell of a lot better than chicken, though actually I don't prefer it to porterhouse.'"

"He said that?" asked the barkeep, reaching for another drink under the bar.

"He said that," answered Mel. "Give me another beer."

The barkeep gave Mel another beer. Mel said, "Well, I still thought that he was joking, you know, so I said, 'All right, let me see your freezer.' And Al says, 'Sure—over here.' And he pulls back the lid and there's the torso in there, a leg and a half, two arms and the head. It's chopped up like that. It looks very sanitary, but it still doesn't look so good to me. The head is looking up at us and the eyes are open and blue, and the tongue is sticking out of the head—it's frozen to the lower lip.

" 'Jesus Christ, Al,' I say to him, 'you're a killer—this is unbelievable, this is sickening!'

" 'Grow up,' he says, 'they kill people by the millions in wars and give out medals for it. Half the people in this world are gonna starve to death while we sit around and watch it on tv.'

"I tell you, Carl, those kitchen walls began to spin, I kept seeing that head, those arms, that chopped-up leg . . . There's something so quiet about a murdered thing, somehow you get to thinking a murdered thing should keep screaming, I don't know.

"Anyhow, I walked over to the kitchen sink and began vomiting. I vomited for a long time. Then I told Al that I had to get out of there. Wouldn't you want to get out of there, Carl?"

"Fast," said Carl. "Very fast."

"Well, Al got in front of the door and he said, 'Listen—that wasn't murder. Nothing's murder. All you've got to do is break through the ideas they've loaded on us and you're a free man—*free*, you understand?'

" 'Get the hell away from that door, Al—I'm getting out of here!'

"He grabs me by the shirt and starts to rip my shirt. I hit him in the face but he keeps ripping at my shirt. I hit him again and again, but he doesn't seem to feel anything. The Rams are still on tv. I step back from the door and then his wife runs up, she grabs me and starts to kiss me. I don't know what to do. She's a powerfully built woman. She knows all these nurses' tricks. I try to push her off but can't. Her mouth is on mine, she's as crazy as he is. I begin to get a hard-on, I can't help it. Her face isn't so great but she has these legs and this big ass and she has on the tightest dress possible. She tastes like boiled onions and her tongue is fat and full of saliva, but she's changed into this new dress—green—and as I pull the dress up I see her petticoat, blood-colored, and it really heats me up and I look over and Al has his cock out and watching.

"I threw her on the couch and soon we were at it, Al standing over us and breathing heavily. We all made it together, a real trio, then I got up and began getting my clothes straight. I went into the bathroom and threw water on my face, combed my hair and came out. When I did they were both sitting on the couch watching the football game. Al had a beer open for me and I sat down and drank it and smoked a cigarette. Then that was all.

"I got up and said I was going. They both said goodbye and Al told me to give them a call anytime. Then I was out of the apartment and into the street, and then I was in my car and driving away. And that was it."

60

"You didn't go to the police?" asked the barkeep.

"Well, you know, Carl, it's hard—they kind of adopted me into the family. It wasn't as if they were trying to hide anything from me."

"The way I look at it is that you're an accessory to a murder."

"But what I got to thinking, Carl, is that those people really didn't seem to be *bad* people. I've seen people I disliked a lot more who never killed anything. I don't know, it's really confusing. I even think of that guy in the freezer as some kind of big frozen rabbit . . ."

The barkeep pulled the Luger out from under the bar and pointed it at Mel.

"Okay," he said, "you just freeze while I call the police."

"Look, Carl—this thing isn't for you to decide."

"The *hell* it isn't! I'm a citizen! You assholes just can't go around popping people into freezers. I may be next!"

"Look, Carl, look at me! I want to tell you something . . ."

"Okay, go ahead."

"It was just bullshit."

"You mean what you told me?"

"Yeah, it was just bullshit. One big joke. I sucked you in. Now put your gun away and pour us both a scotch and water."

"That story wasn't bullshit."

"I just told you it was."

"That was no bullshit story—there was too much detail. Nobody tells a story like that. That's no joke. Nobody jokes that way."

"I tell you it was *bullshit*, Carl."

"There's no way I can believe that."

Carl reached over to his left to slide the phone down toward him. The phone had been sitting on the bar. When Carl reached to his left Mel grabbed the beer bottle and got Carl across the face with it. Carl dropped the gun and held his face and Mel jumped over the bar, hit him again—this time behind the ear—and Carl dropped. Mel picked up the Luger, aimed carefully, squeezed the trigger once, then put the gun in a brown paper bag, jumped back over the bar, walked out the entrance and he was on the boulevard. The parking meter read "expired" in front of his car, but there was no ticket. He got in and drove off.

HAVE YOU READ PIRANDELLO?

My girlfriend had suggested that I move out of her house, a very large house, nice and comfortable, with a backyard a block long, leaking pipes, and frogs and crickets and cats. Anyway, I was out, as one gets out of such situations—with honor, courage, and expectation. I placed an ad in one of the underground papers:

> Writer: needs place where the sound of a typewriter is more welcome than the laugh track on "I Love Lucy." $100 a month o.k. Privacy a must.

I had a month to move while my girlfriend was in Colorado for her yearly family reunion. I lay around in bed and waited for the phone to ring. Finally it rang. It was a guy who wanted me to babysit his three children whenever the "creative urge" overcame either him or his wife. Free room and board, and I could write whenever the creative urge was not on them. I told him I would think about it. The phone rang again two hours later. "Well?" he asked. "No," I said. "Well," he said, "do you know a pregnant woman in trouble?" I told him I would try to find him one and hung up.

The next day the phone rang again. "I read your ad," she said. "I teach yoga." "Oh?" "Yes, I teach exercise and meditation." "Oh?" "You're a writer?" "Yes." "What do you write about?" "Oh, god, I don't know. Bad as it sounds: Life . . . I guess." "That doesn't sound bad. Does it include sex?" "Doesn't life?" "Sometimes. Sometimes not." "I see." "What's your name?" "Henry Chinaski." "Have you ever been published?" "Yes." "Well, I have a master bedroom you can have for $100. With a private entrance." "Sounds good." "Have you read

Pirandello?" "Yes." "Have you read Swinburne?" "Everybody has."
"Have you read Herman Hesse?" "Yes, but I'm not homosexual."
"Do you hate homosexuals?" "No, but I don't love them." "What
about blacks?" "What about blacks?" "What do you think of them?"
"They're fine." "Are you prejudiced?" "Everybody is." "What do you
think God is?" "White hair, a stringy beard and no pecker." "What
do you think about love?" "I don't think about it." "You're a smart-
ass. Here, I'll give you my address. Come out and see me."

I took down the address and lay around a couple more days
watching the soaps in the morning and the spy thrillers at night,
plus the boxing matches. The phone rang again. It was the lady.

"You didn't come." "I've been engrossed." "Are you in love?" "Yes,
I'm writing my new novel." "Lots of sex?" "Some of the time." "Are
you a good lover?" "Most men like to think they are. I'm probably
good but not great." "Do you eat pussy?" "Yes." "Good." "Your room
still available?" "Yes, the master bedroom. Do you really go down
on a woman?" "Hell yes. But everybody does now. This is 1982 and
I am 62 years old. You can get a man 30 years younger and he can
do the same thing. Probably better." "You'd be surprised."

I walked over to the refrigerator and got a beer and a smoke. When
I picked up the receiver she was still there. "What's your name?"
I asked. She told me some fancy name which I promptly forgot.

"I've been reading your stuff," she said. "You're really a powerful
writer. You have a lot of shit in you but you've got a way of working on people's emotions."

"You're right. I'm not great but I'm different."

"How do you go down on a woman?"

"Now wait . . ."

"No, tell me."

"Well, it's an art."

"Yes, it is."

"How do you begin?" "With a brush stroke, lightly." "Of course,
of course. Then, after you begin?" "Yes, well, there are techniques
. . ." "What techniques?" "The first touch usually dulls the sensitivity
in that area so that you can't return to it with the same effec-
tiveness." "What the hell do you mean?" "You know what I mean."
"You're making me hot." "This is clinical." "This is sexual. You're
making me hot." "I don't know what else to say." "What does a man
do then?" "You let your own enjoyment guide your exploration.

It's different each time." "What do you mean?" "I mean sometimes it's a bit gross, sometimes it's tender, whichever way you feel." "Tell me." "Well, everything ends up at the clit." "Say that word again." "What?" "Clit." "Clit, clit, clit . . ." "Do you suck it? Nibble it?" "Of course." "You're making me hot." "Sorry." "You can have the master bedroom. You like privacy?" "Like I told you." "Tell me about my clit." "All clits are different." "It's not private here right now. They're building a retaining wall. But they'll be through in a couple of days. You'll like it here."

I took her address down again, hung up and went to bed. The phone rang. I walked over and picked it up and took it back to bed with me. "What do you mean, all clits are different?" "I mean different in size and response to stimuli." "Did you ever find one you couldn't stimulate?" "Not yet." "Listen, why don't you just come see me now?" "I've got an old car. It won't make it up the canyon." "Take the freeway and park in the lot at the Hidden Hills turnoff. I'll meet you there." "O.K."

I hung up, got dressed and got into my car. I took the freeway to the Hidden Hills turnoff, found the parking lot and sat there and waited. Twenty minutes went by and then a fat lady in a green dress drove up. She was in a white 1982 Caddy. All her front teeth were capped. "Are you the one?" she asked.

"I'm the one."

"Jesus Christ. You don't look so hot."

"You don't look so hot either."

"All right. Come on."

I got out of my car and into hers. Her dress was very short. On the fat thigh nearest me was a small tattoo that looked like a messenger boy standing on top of a dog.

"I'm not paying you anything," she said.

"That's all right."

"You don't look like a writer."

"For that I'm thankful."

"In fact, you don't look like a guy who can do anything . . ."

"Many things I can't do."

"But you sure talk some shit on the phone. I was playing with myself. Were you playing with yourself?"

"No."

We drove in silence after that. I had two cigarettes left and smoked both of them. Then I turned on her radio and listened to the music. Her place had a long curving driveway and the garage doors opened automatically as we drove in. She unhitched her seatbelt and then suddenly flung her arms around me. Her mouth looked like an open bottle of red india ink. The tongue came out. We rolled back against the seat, trapped like that. Then it ended and we got out. "Come on," she said. I followed her up a path lined with rosebushes. "I'm not going to pay you anything," she said, "not a fucking thing." "That's all right," I said. She got her key out of her purse, unlocked the door and I followed her in.

STROKES TO NOWHERE

Meg and Tony got his wife to the airport. After Dolly was airborne they stopped in the airport bar for a drink. Meg had a whiskey and soda. Tony had a scotch and water.

"Your wife trusts you," said Meg.

"Yeh," said Tony.

"I wonder if I can trust you?"

"Don't you like to be fucked?"

"That's not the point."

"What's the point?"

"The point is that Dolly and I are friends."

"*We* can be friends."

"Not that way."

"Be modern. It's the modern age. People swing. They're uninhibited. They fuck from the ceiling. They screw dogs, babies, chickens, fish . . ."

"I like to choose. I have to care."

"That's so damned corny. The caring is already built-in. Then if you cultivate the caring long enough the next thing you know you think it's love."

"O.K., what's wrong with love, Tony?"

"Love is a form of prejudice. You love what you need, you love what makes you feel good, you love what is convenient. How can you say you love one person when there are ten thousand people in the world that you would love more if you ever met them? But you'll never meet them."

"All right, so we do the best we can."

"Granted. But we must still realize that love is just the result of a chance encounter. Most people make too much of it. On these grounds a good fuck is not to be entirely scorned."

"But that's the result of a chance meeting too."

"You're damned right. Drink up. We'll have another."

"You've got a good line, Tony, but it's not going to work."

"Well," said Tony, nodding the bartender over, "I'm not going to grieve about that either . . ."

It was a Saturday evening and they went back to Tony's place and turned on the tv. There wasn't a hell of a lot on. They drank some Tuborg and talked over the sound of the set.

"You ever heard the one," asked Tony, "about horses being too smart to bet on people?"

"No."

"Well, anyhow, it's a saying. You're not going to believe this but I had a dream the other night. I was down in the stables and a horse came to get me and give me a workout. There was a monkey with his arms and legs around my neck and he smelled of cheap wine. It was 6 a.m. and the cold wind blew in from the San Gabriel mountains. What's more it was foggy. They worked me three furlongs in 52, handily. Then they hot-walked me for 30 minutes and walked me back to the barn. A horse came in and gave me two hardboiled eggs, grapefruit, toast and milk. Then I was in a race. The stands were packed with horses. It looked like a Saturday. I was in the fifth race. I came in first and paid $32.40. That was some dream, wasn't it?"

"I'll say," said Meg. She crossed her legs. She had on a miniskirt but no pantyhose. Her boots covered the calves of her legs. Her thighs were bare, and full. "That was some dream." She was 30. Lipstick ever so faintly glistened on her lips. Brunette, very dark, long hair. No powder, no perfume. Never fingerprinted. Born in the northern part of Maine. One hundred twenty pounds.

Tony got up and got two more bottles of beer. When he came back Meg said: "A strange dream, but many of them are. It's when strange things happen in life, it makes you wonder . . ."

"Like?"

"Like my brother Damion. He was always poking into books . . . mysticism, yoga, all that shit. Come into a room he'd be as apt to be standing on his head in his jockey shorts as anything else.

He even managed a couple of trips east . . . India, somewhere else. Came back hollow-cheeked and half-crazy, weighing about 76 pounds. But he kept at it. He meets this guy Ram Da Beetle, or some similar name. Ram Da Beetle's got a big tent down near San Diego and he's charging these suckers $175 for a five-day seminar. The tent is pitched on a cliff overlooking the sea. This old girl the Beetle is sleeping with, she owns the land, she lets him use it. Damion claims Ram Da Beetle gave him the final revelation he needed. And it was a shocker. I'm living in this small apartment in Detroit and he shows up and works the shocker on me . . ."

Tony looked higher up Meg's legs and said, "Damion's shocker? What shocker?"

"O.K., you know, he just *appears* . . ." Meg picked up her Tuborg.

"He came to visit you?"

"You might say that. Let me put it to you simply: Damion can dematerialize his body."

"He can? Then what happens?"

"He appears someplace else."

"Just like that?"

"Just like that."

"Long distances?"

"He came all the way from India to Detroit, to my apartment in Detroit."

"How long did it take?"

"I don't know. Ten seconds, maybe."

"Ten seconds . . . ummm."

They sat there looking at each other. Meg sat on the couch and Tony sat across from her.

"Listen, Meg, you really give me the hots. My wife would never know."

"No, Tony."

"Where's your brother now?"

"He took my apartment in Detroit. He works in a shoe factory."

"Listen, why can't he get into a bank vault, take the money and get on out of there? He can use his talents. Why work in a shoe factory?"

"He says such a talent can't be used to further the purposes of evil."

"I see. Listen, Meg, let's forget your brother."

Tony walked over and sat on the couch next to Meg.

"You know, Meg, what *is* evil, and what we are *taught* is evil, can be two very different things. Society teaches us that certain things are evil in order to keep us subservient."

"Like robbing banks?"

"Like fucking without going through all the proper channels."

Tony grabbed Meg and kissed her. She didn't resist. He kissed her again. Her tongue slid into his mouth.

"I still don't think we should do it, Tony."

"You kiss like you want to."

"I haven't had a man for months, Tony. It's hard to resist but Dolly and I are friends. I hate to do it to her."

"You won't be doing it to her, you'll be doing it to me."

"You know what I mean." Tony kissed her again, this time a long full kiss. Their bodies pressed together.

"Let's go to the bedroom, Meg."

She followed him in. Tony began undressing, throwing his clothes over a chair. Meg went into the bathroom, which was just off the bedroom. She sat down and pissed with the door open.

"I don't want to get pregnant and I don't take the pill."

"Don't worry."

"Don't worry why?"

"I got my strings cut."

"All you guys say that."

"It's true, I'm cut."

Meg got up and flushed.

"Suppose you want a baby sometime?"

"I don't want a baby sometime."

"I think it's awful for a man to get his strings cut."

"Oh, for Christ's sake, Meg, stop the moralizing and come to bed."

Meg walked into the room naked. "I mean, Tony, I kind of think of it as a crime against nature."

"How about abortion? Is that a crime against nature too?"

"Of course. It's murder."

"How about a rubber? How about masturbation?"

"Oh, Tony, it's not the same thing."

"Get into bed before we die of old age."

Meg got on in and Tony grabbed her. "Ah, you feel good. Kind of like rubber filled with air . . ."

"Where'd you get that thing, Tony? Dolly never told me about that thing . . . it's huge!"

"Why should she tell you?"

"You're right. Just put that damned thing into me!"

"Just wait now, just wait!"

"Come on, I want it!"

"How about Dolly? Do you think it will be the right thing to do?"

"She's grieving over her dying mother! She can't use it! I can use it!"

"All right! All right!"

Tony mounted her and put it in.

"That's it, Tony! Now move it, move it!"

Tony moved it. He moved it slowly and steadily like the arm of an oil pump. Flub, flub, flub, flub.

"Oh, you son of a bitch! Oh my god, you son of a bitch!"

"All right now, Meg! Get out of that bed! You are committing a crime against native decency and trust!"

Tony felt a hand on his shoulder and then he felt himself being pulled off. He rolled over and looked up. There was a man standing there in a green t-shirt and bluejeans.

"Listen, you," said Tony, "what the hell are you doing in my house?"

"It's Damion!" said Meg.

"Clothe thyself, little sister! The shame still radiates from thy body!"

"Look here, motherfucker," said Tony from where he lay on the bed.

Meg was in the bathroom dressing, "I'm sorry, Damion, I am sorry!"

"I see I arrived from Detroit just in time," said Damion. "Another few minutes and I would have been too late."

"Another ten seconds," said Tony.

"You might as well clothe yourself too, my man," said Damion looking down at Tony.

"Mother," said Tony, "I happen to *live* here. I don't know *who* let you in. But I figure if I want to lay here balls naked, I've got a right."

"Hurry, Meg," said Damion, "I will take you out of this nest of sin."

"Listen, mother," said Tony, getting up and slipping into his jocks, "your sister wanted it and I wanted it and that's two votes to one."

"Ta-ta," said Damion.

"Ta-ta, nothing," said Tony. "She was about to get her rocks off and I was about to get my rocks off and you come bursting in here and interfere with a decent democratic decision, stopping a good old-fashioned horse-fuck!"

"Pack your things, Meg. I'm taking you home immediately."

"Yes, Damion!"

"I got a good mind to bust you up, fuck-killer!"

"Please restrain yourself. I abhor violence!"

Tony swung. Damion was gone.

"Over here, Tony." Damion was standing over by the bathroom door. Tony rushed him. He vanished again.

"Over here, Tony." Damion was standing on top of the bed, shoes and all.

Tony rushed across the room, leaped, found nothing, flew over the bed and fell to the floor. He got up and looked around. "Damion! Oh, Damion, you cheap-ass, tinhorn, shoe-factory Superman, where are you? Oh, Damion! Here, Damion! Come to me, Damion!"

Tony felt the blow on the back of his neck. There was a flash of red and the faint sound of one trumpet playing. Then he fell forward on the rug.

It was the telephone that brought him to consciousness some time later. He managed to get to the night stand where the phone sat, lifted the receiver and slumped down on the bed.

"Tony?"

"Yes?"

"Is this Tony?"

"Yes."

"This is Dolly."

"Hey, Dolly, whatcha say, Dolly?"

"Don't be funny, Tony. Mother died."

"Mother?"

"Yes, my mother. Tonight."

"I'm sorry."

"I'll stay for the funeral. I'll be home after the funeral."

Tony hung up. He saw the morning paper on the floor. He picked it up and stretched out on the bed. The war in the Falklands was still on. Both sides charged violations of this and that. There was still firing. Wouldn't that god damned war ever end?

Tony got up and walked into the kitchen. He found some salami and liverwurst in the refrigerator. He made a salami and liverwurst sandwich with hot mustard, relish, onion and tomato. He found one bottle of Tuborg left. He drank the Tuborg and ate the salami and liverwurst sandwich at the breakfastnook table. Then he lit a cigarette and sat there thinking, well, maybe the old lady left a little money, that would be nice, that would be damned nice. A man deserved a little luck after a rough night like this.

SOME MOTHER

Eddie's mother had horseteeth and I did too and I remember once we walked up a hill together on the way to the store and she said, "Henry, we both need braces for our teeth. We look awful!" I walked proudly up the hill with her and she had on a tight yellow print dress, flowered, and she had on high heels and she wiggled and her heels went *click, click, click* on the cement. I thought, I'm walking with Eddie's mother and she's walking with me and we're walking up the hill together. That was all—I walked into the store to buy a loaf of bread for my parents and she purchased her things. That was all.

I liked to go to Eddie's place. His mother always sat in a chair with a drink in her hand and she crossed her legs real high and you could see where the stockings ended and where the flesh began. I liked Eddie's mother, she was a real lady. When I walked in she'd say, "Hi, Henry!" and smile and she wouldn't pull her skirt down. Eddie's father would say hello too. He was a big guy and he'd be sitting there with a drink in his hand too. Jobs weren't easy to get in 1933 and besides, Eddie's father couldn't work. He'd been an aviator in World War I and had been shot down. He had wires in his arms instead of bone, and so he sat there and drank with Eddie's mother. It was dark in there where they were drinking but Eddie's mother laughed often.

Eddie and I made model airplanes, cheap balsa wood jobs. They wouldn't fly, we just moved them through the air with our hands. Eddie had a Spad and I had a Fokker. We'd seen "Hell's Angels" with Jean Harlow. I couldn't see that Jean Harlow was any sexier than

Eddie's mother. Of course, I didn't talk about Eddie's mother to Eddie. Then I noticed that Eugene started coming over. Eugene was another guy with a Spad but I could talk about Eddie's mother to him. When we got the chance. We had some good dogfights—two Spads against a Fokker. I did the best I could but usually I got shot down. Whenever I got into a real bad spot I'd pull an Immelman. We read the old flying magazines, *Flying Aces* was best. I even wrote some letters to the editor which he answered. The Immelman, he wrote me, was almost impossible. The stress on the wings was just too great. But sometimes I had to use the Immelman, especially with a guy on my tail. It usually tore my wings off and I had to bail out.

When we got the chance away from Eddie we'd talk about Eddie's mother.

"Jesus, she's got *some* legs."

"And she doesn't mind showing them."

"Watch out, here comes Eddie."

Eddie had no idea we were talking about his mother that way. I was a little ashamed of it but I couldn't help it. I certainly didn't want him to think of my mother that way. Of course, my mother didn't look like that. Nobody else's mother looked like that. Maybe those horseteeth had something to do with it. I mean, you'd look and see the horseteeth and they were a bit yellow and then you'd look down and see those legs crossed high, one foot flicking and kicking. Yes, I had horseteeth too.

Well, Eugene and I kept going over there and having the dogfights and I'd do my Immelmans and my wings would get ripped off. Although we had another game and Eddie played that one too. We were stunt flyers and racers. We'd go out and take big chances but somehow we always made it back. Often we landed in our own front yards. We each had a house and we each had a wife and our wives would be waiting for us. We'd describe how our wives would be dressed. They didn't wear much. Eugene's wore the least. In fact, she had a dress with a big hole cut right into the front of it. She'd meet Eugene at the door that way. My wife wasn't quite that bold, but she didn't wear much either. We all made love all the time. We made love to our wives all the time. They just couldn't get enough. While we were out stunting and racing and risking our lives they'd be in those houses waiting and waiting for us. And they just loved us, they didn't love anybody else. Sometimes we'd try to forget about them and go back to the dogfights. It was like Eddie said: when we were talking about women all we did was lay on the grass and we didn't do anything else. The most we would do, Eddie would say, "Hey, I got one!" And then I'd roll off my belly and show him mine and then Eugene would show his. That's how most of our afternoons went. Eddie's mother and father would be in there drinking and once in a while we'd hear Eddie's mother laugh.

One day Eugene and I went over there and we hollered for Eddie and Eddie didn't come out. "Hey, Eddie, for Christ's sake, come on out!" Eddie didn't come out.

"Something's wrong in there," Eugene said, "I know there's something wrong in there."

"Maybe somebody got murdered."

"We'd better look in there."

"You think we should?"

"We'd better."

The screen door pulled open and we walked in. It was as dark as usual. Then we heard a single word:

"*Shit!*"

Eddie's mother was lying on the bed in the bedroom and she was drunk. Her legs were up and her dress had fallen way back. Eugene grabbed my arm. "Jesus, look at that!"

It looked good, my god it looked good but I was too scared to appreciate it. Suppose somebody came in and found us there looking? Her dress was way back and she was drunk, those thighs exposed, you could almost see the panties.

"Come on, Eugene, let's get out of here!"

"No, let's look. I want to look at her. Look at all that showing!"

It reminded me of the time I was hitchhiking and a woman picked me up. She had her skirt up high around her waist, well, almost up around her waist. I looked away, I looked down, and I was scared. She just talked to me as I looked through the windshield and I answered her questions, "Where are you going?" "Nice day, isn't it?" But I was scared. I didn't know what to do but I was afraid that if I did it, there'd be trouble, that she'd scream or call the police. So now and then I just sneaked a look and then I turned my eyes away. She finally let me out.

I was scared about Eddie's mother too.

"Listen, Eugene, I'm leaving."

"She's drunk, she doesn't even know we're here."

"Son of a bitch left," she said from the bed. "Left and took the kid, my baby . . ."

"She's talking," I said.

"She's knocked out," said Eugene, "she doesn't know what the hell."

He moved toward the bed. "Watch this."

He took her skirt and pulled it further back. He pulled it back so you could see the panties. They were pink.

"Eugene, I'm leaving!"

"Chicken!"

Eugene just stood there staring at her thighs and panties. He stood there a long time. Then he took out his cock. I heard Eddie's mother moan. She shifted on the bed just a little. Eugene moved closer. Then he touched her thigh with the end of his cock. She moaned again. Then Eugene spurted. He shot his sperm all over her thigh and there seemed to be plenty of it. You could see it running down her leg. Then Eddie's mother said, *"Shit!"* and she suddenly sat up in bed. Eugene ran past me out the door and I turned and ran too. Eugene ran into the icebox in the kitchen, bounced off and jumped out the screen door. I followed him and we ran down the street. We ran all the way to my house, down the driveway, and we ran into the garage and pulled the doors shut.

"You think she saw us?" I asked.

"I don't know. I shot all over her pink panties."

"You're crazy. What'd you do it for?"

"I got hot. I couldn't help it. I couldn't help myself."

"We'll go to jail."

"You didn't do anything. I shot all over her leg."

"I was watching."

"Listen," said Eugene, "I think I'll go home."

"All right, go on."

I watched him walk up the driveway and then cross the street to his place. I walked out of the garage. I walked through the back porch and into my bedroom and I sat there and waited. Nobody was home. I went into the bathroom and locked the door and I thought about Eddie's mother lying on the bed like that. Only I

78

imagined I got her pink panties off and I got it in. And she liked it . . .

I waited the rest of the afternoon and I waited all through dinner for something to happen but nothing happened. I went to my bedroom after dinner and sat there and waited. Then it was time to go to sleep and I lay there in bed and I waited. I heard my father snoring in the other room and I still waited. Then I slept.

The next day was Saturday and I saw Eugene on his front lawn with a beebee gun. There were two large palm trees in front of his house and he was trying to kill some of the sparrows who lived up there. He'd already gotten two of them. They had three cats and every time one of the sparrows fell to the grass, wings flopping, one of the cats would rush up and scoop him off.

"Nothing's happened," I said to Eugene.

"If it hasn't happened by now, it won't," he said. "I should have fucked her. I'm sorry now I didn't fuck her."

He got another sparrow and down it came and a very fat grey cat with greenyellow eyes picked it up and was off with it behind the hedge. I walked back across the street to my place. My old man was waiting on the front porch. He looked angry. "Listen, I want you to get busy mowing the lawn! *Now!*"

I walked to the garage and pulled out the mower. First I mowed the driveway, then I went out to the front lawn. The mower was stiff and old and it was hard work. My old man stood there, looking angry, watching me, as I pushed the mower through the tangled grass.

SCUM GRIEF

The poet Victor Valoff was not a very good poet. He had a local reputation, was liked by the ladies and supported by his wife. He was continually giving readings at local bookstores and he was often heard on the Public Radio Station. He read in a loud and dramatic voice but the pitch never varied. Victor was always at climax. That's what attracted the ladies, I guess. Certain of his lines, if taken separately, seemed to have power, but when all the lines were considered as a whole, you knew that Victor was saying nothing, only saying it loudly.

But Vicki, like most ladies, being easily charmed by fools, insisted upon hearing Valoff read. It was a hot Friday night in a Feminist-Lesbian-Revolutionary bookshop. No admission. Valoff read for free. And there would be a display of his art work after the reading. His art work was very modern. A stroke or two, usually red, and a bit of an epigram in a contrasting color. Some piece of wisdom would be inscribed on it like:

> Green heaven come home to me,
> I weep grey, gray, grey, gray . . .

Valoff was intelligent. He knew there were two ways to spell grey.

Photos of Tim Leary hung about. IMPEACH REAGAN signs. I didn't mind the IMPEACH REAGAN signs. Valoff rose and walked to the platform, a half bottle of beer in his hand.

"Look," said Vicki, "look at that face! How he has suffered!"

"Yeah," I said, "and now I'm going to suffer."

Valoff did have a fairly interesting face — compared to most poets. But compared to most poets almost everybody has.

Victor Valoff began:

> "East of the Suez of my heart
> begins a buzzing buzzing buzzing
> sombre still, still sombre
> and suddenly Summer comes home
> straight on through like a
> Quarterback sneak on the one yard line
> of my heart!"

Victor screamed the last line and as he did so somebody near me said, *"Beautiful!"* It was a local feminist poet who had grown tired of blacks and now fucked a doberman in her bedroom. She had braided red hair, dull eyes, and played a mandolin while she read her work. Most of her work involved something about a dead baby's footprint in the sand. She was married to a doctor who was never around (at least he had the good sense not to attend poetry readings). He gave her a large allowance to support her poetry and to feed the doberman.

Valoff continued:

> "Docks and ducks and derivative day
> Ferment behind my forehead
> in a most unforgiving way
> o, in a most unforgiving way.
> I sway through the light and darkness . . ."

"I've got to agree with him there," I told Vicki.
"Please be quiet," she answered.

> "With one thousand pistols and one
> thousand hopes
> I step onto the porch of my mind
> to murder one thousand Popes!"

I found my half pint, uncapped it and took a good hit.
"Listen," said Vicki, "you always get drunk at these readings. Can't you contain yourself?"
"I get drunk at my own readings," I said. "I can't stand my stuff either."

"*Gummed mercy,*" Valoff went on, "*that's what we are, gummed mercy, gummed gummed gummed mercy . . .*"

"He's going to say something about a raven," I said.

"*Gummed mercy,*" continued Valoff, "*and the raven forevermore . . .*"

I laughed. Valoff recognized the laugh. He looked down at me. "Ladies and gentlemen," he said, "in the audience tonight we have the poet Henry Chinaski."

Little hisses were heard. They knew me. "Sexist pig!" "Drunk!" "Motherfucker!" I took another drink. "Please continue, Victor," I said. He did.

> ". . . conditioned under the hump of valor
> the ersatz imminent piddling rectangle is
> no more than a gene in Genoa
> a quadruplet Quetzalcoatal
> and the Chink cries bittersweet and barbaric
> into her muff!"

"It's beautiful," said Vicki, "but what's he talking about?"

"He's talking about eating pussy."

"I thought so. He's a beautiful man."

"I hope he eats pussy better than he writes."

> "grief, christ, my grief,
> that scum grief,
> stars and stripes of grief,
> waterfalls of grief
> tides of grief,
> grief at discount
> everywhere . . ."

" 'That scum grief,' " I said, "I like that."

"He's stopped talking about eating pussy?"

"Yes, now he says he doesn't feel good."

> ". . . a Baker's dozen, a cousin's cousin,
> let in the streptomycin
> and, propitious, gorge my
> gonfalon.
> I dream the carnival plasma
> across frantic leather . . ."

"Now what's he saying?" asked Vicki.

"He's saying he's getting ready to eat pussy again."

"Again?"

Victor read some more and I drank some more. Then he called a ten minute intermission and the audience went up and gathered around the podium. Vicki went up too. It was hot in there and I walked out into the street to cool off. There was a bar a half block away. I got a beer. It wasn't too crowded. There was a basketball game on tv. I watched the game. Of course, I didn't care who won. My only thought was, my god, how they run up and down, up and down. I'll bet their jockstraps are soaking wet, I'll bet their assholes smell something awful. I had another beer and then walked back to the poetry hole. Valoff was already back on. I could hear him half a block down the street:

> "Choke, Columbia, and the dead horses of
> my soul
> greet me at the gates
> greet me sleeping, Historians
> see this tenderest Past
> leapt over with
> geisha dreams, drilled dead with
> importunity!"

I found my seat next to Vicki. "What's he saying now?" she asked me.

"He's really not saying very much. Basically what he's saying is that he can't sleep nights. He ought to find a job."

"He's saying he ought to find a job?"

"No, I'm saying that."

> ". . . the lemming and the falling star are
> brothers, the contest of the lake
> is the El Dorado of my
> heart. come take my head, come take my
> eyes, larrup me with larkspur . . ."

"Now what's he saying?"

"He's saying he needs a big fat woman to kick the shit out of him."

"Don't be funny. Does he really say that?"

"We both say that."

> "... I could eat the emptiness,
> I could fire cartridges of love into the dark
> I could beg India for your recessive
> mulch . . ."

Well, Victor went on and on, and on. One sane person got up and walked out. The remainder of us stayed.

> "... I say, drag the dead gods through the
> crabgrass!
> I say the palm is lucrative
> I say, look, look, look
> around us:
> all love is ours
> all life is ours
> the sun is our dog at the end of a leash
> there is nothing that can defeat us!
> fuck the salmon!
> we need only reach,
> we need only drag ourselves out of
> obvious graves,
> the earth, the dirt,
> the plaid hope of looming grafts to our very
> senses. We have nothing to take and nothing to
> give, we need only to
> begin, begin, begin . . . !"

"Thank you very much," said Victor Valoff, "for being here."

The applause was very loud. They always applauded. Victor was immense in his glory. He lifted his same bottle of beer. He even managed to blush. Then he grinned, a very human grin. The ladies loved it. I took a last hit on my bottle of whiskey.

They were up around Victor. He was giving his autograph and answering questions. His art show would be next. I managed to get Vicki out of there and we walked along the street back to the car.

"He reads powerfully," she said.

"Yes, he has a good voice."

"What do you think of his work?"

"I think it's pure."

"I think you're jealous."

"Let's stop here for a drink," I said. "There's a basketball game."

"All right," she said.

We were lucky. The game was still on. We sat down.

"Oh boy," said Vicki, "look at the long legs on those guys!"

"Now you're talking," I said. "What'll you have?"

"Scotch and soda."

I ordered two scotch and sodas and we watched the game. Those guys ran up and down, up and down. Wonderful. They seemed very excited about something. The place was hardly crowded at all. It seemed the best part of the night.

NOT QUITE BERNADETTE

I wrapped the towel around my bloody cock and phoned the doctor's office. I had to set the receiver down and dial with one hand while holding the towel with the other. Even as I dialed, a red stain began to blossom through the towel. I got the doctor's receptionist.

"Oh, Mr. Chinaski, what is it now? Did your earplugs get lost in your ears again?"

"No, this is a bit more serious. I need an early appointment."

"How about tomorrow afternoon at 4 p.m.?"

"Miss Simms, this is an emergency."

"What is its nature?"

"Please, I must see the doctor *now*."

"All right. Come on over and we'll try to work you in."

"Thank you, Miss Simms."

I fashioned a temporary bandage by ripping up a clean shirt and winding it about my penis. Luckily I had a bit of adhesive tape but it was old and yellow and didn't grip very well. I had some problem getting my pants on. I looked like I had a gigantic hard-on. I was only able to partly zip up my pants. I made my way to my car, got in and drove to the doctor's office. Getting out in the parking lot I shocked two old ladies coming out of the optometrist's who was downstairs. I managed to get in the elevator alone and go to the third floor. I saw somebody coming up the hallway, turned my back to them and feigned drinking from the water fountain. Then I walked down the hall and into the doctor's office. The waiting room was full of people with no real problems—gonorrhea, herpes, syphilis, cancer, and so forth. I walked up to the receptionist.

"Ah, Mr. Chinaski . . ."

"Please, Miss Simms, no *jokes!* This *is* an emergency, I assure you. Hurry!"

"You can go in as soon as the doctor has finished with his present patient."

I stood at the partition that separated the receptionist from the rest of us and waited. As soon as the patient emerged I ran into the doctor's office.

"Chinaski, what is it?"

"Emergency, doctor."

"I took off my shoes and stockings, pants and shorts, flung myself back upon the table.

"What do you have here? That's quite a bandage."

I didn't answer. I had my eyes closed and could feel the doctor tugging at the bandage.

"You know," I said, "I knew a girl in a small town. She was in her early teens and she was playing around with a coke bottle. She got it stuck up there and couldn't get it out. She had to go to the doctor. You know how small towns are. The word got out. Her whole life was ruined. She was shunned. Nobody would touch her. The most beautiful girl in town. She finally married a midget in a wheelchair who had some kind of palsy."

"That's old stuff," said my doctor, yanking the last of the bandage off. "How did this happen to you?"

"Well, her name was Bernadette, 22, married. She has long blonde hair that keeps falling into her face and has to be brushed away . . ."

"Twenty-two?"

"Yes, she had on bluejeans . . ."

"You're rather badly cut here."

"She knocked on the door. She asked if she could come in. 'Sure,' I said. 'I've had it,' she said and she ran into my bathroom, half closed the door, pulled down her jeans and panties, sat down and began to piss. OOH! CHRIST!"

"Take it easy. I'm sterilizing the wound."

"You know, doctor, wisdom comes at a hell of an hour—when youth is gone, the storm is over and the girls have gone home."

"Quite true."

"OW! OH! JESUS!"

"Please. This must be properly cleaned."

"She came out and told me that last night at her party I hadn't solved the problem of her unhappy love affair. That instead I had gotten everybody drunk, had fallen into a rose bush. That I had ripped my pants, fallen over backwards, hit my head on a large stone. Somebody named Willy had carried me home and my pants fell down and then my shorts, but that I hadn't solved the love affair problem. She said that the affair was over anyhow, and at least I had said some heavy things."

"Where did you meet this girl?"

"I gave a poetry reading in Venice. Met her afterwards in the bar next door."

"Can you recite me a poem?"

"No, doctor. Anyhow, she said 'I've *had* it, man!' She sat on the couch. I sat in a chair across from her. She drank her beer and told me about it: 'I love him, you know, but I can't get any *contact*, he won't talk. I tell him, *talk* to me! But, by god, he won't talk. He says, "It's not you, it's something else." And that ends that.'"

"Now, Chinaski, I'm going to stitch you up. It won't be pleasant."

"Yes, doctor. Anyhow, she got to talking about her life. She said she'd been married three times. I said she didn't show that much wear. And she said, 'I don't? Well, I've been in a madhouse twice.' And I said, 'You too?' And she said, 'You been in a madhouse too?' And I said, 'No, just some women I've known.'"

"Now," said the doctor, "just a little thread. That's all it is. Thread. A bit of embroidery work."

"Oh, shit, isn't there another way?"

"No, you're too badly cut."

"She said she got married at 15. They were calling her a whore for going with this guy. Her parents were calling her a whore so she married the guy to spite them. Her mother was a drunk, in and out of madhouses. Her father beat her all the time. OH JESUS! PLEASE GO EASY!"

"Chinaski, you have more trouble with women than any man I've ever met."

"Then she met this dyke. The dyke took her to a homosexual bar. She left the dyke and went off with a homosexual boy. They lived together. They used to argue over makeup. OH! CHRIST! MERCY! She'd steal his lipstick and then he'd steal hers. Then she married him . . ."

"This will take any number of stitches. How did this happen?"

"I'm *telling* you, doctor. They had a child. Then they divorced and he took off and left her with the child. She got a job, hired a babysitter, but the job didn't pay much and after the babysitter's fees there wasn't much left. She had to go out at night and hustle. Ten bucks for a piece of ass. It went on for some time. She wasn't getting anywhere. Then one day at work—she was working for Avon—she started screaming and couldn't seem to stop. They took her to a madhouse. EASY! EASY! PLEASE!"

"What was her name?"

"Bernadette. She got out of the madhouse, came to L.A., met and married Karl. She told me how she liked my poetry and how she admired the way I drove my car on the sidewalk at 60 m.p.h. after my readings. Then she said that she was hungry and she offered to buy me a hamburger and fries, so she drove me to McDonald's. PLEASE, DOCTOR! GO SLOWER OR GET A SHARPER NEEDLE OR SOMETHING!"

"I'm almost finished."

"Well we sat at a table with our hamburgers, french fries, coffee, and then Bernadette told me about her mother. She was worried about her mother. She was also worried about her two sisters. One sister was so unhappy and the other sister was just dull and satisfied. And then there was her boy and she was worried about Karl's relationship with the boy . . ."

The doctor yawned and stitched another stitch.

"I told her that she was carrying too much weight, to let some of those people float for themselves. Then I noticed that she was trembling and I told her I was sorry I had said that. I took one of her hands and began to rub it. Then I rubbed the other one. I slid her hands up my wrists under my coat sleeves. 'I'm sorry,' I told her, 'I guess you just *care*. There's nothing wrong with that.'"

"But how did it happen? This thing?"

"Well, when I walked Bernadette down the steps my hand was around her waist. She still looked like a high school girl—long silken blond hair; a very sensitive and sexy pair of lips. The only way you could tell about the hell was to look into her eyes. They were in a perpetual state of shock."

"Please get to the happening," said the doctor. "I'm almost finished."

"Well, when we got to my place there was some fool standing on the sidewalk with a dog. I told her to drive further up. She double-parked and I pulled her head back and kissed her. I gave her a long one, pulled back, then followed with another. She called me a son of a bitch. I told her to give an old man a break. I kissed her again, a long one. 'That's not a kiss, man,' she said, 'that's sex, that's almost rape!' "

"*Then* it happened?"

"I slid out the door and she said she'd phone me in a week. I walked into my place and *then* it happened."

"How?"

"Can I be frank with you, doctor?"

"Of course."

"Well, looking at her body and face, her hair, her eyes . . . listening to her talk, then the kisses, it had gotten me hot."

"So?"

"So I've got this vase. It's a perfect fit for me. I put it into this vase and started thinking of Bernadette. I was going good when the damn thing broke. I had used it several times before but I suppose this time I was terribly excited. She's such a sexy-looking woman . . ."

"Never never stick that thing into anything made of glass."

"Will I be all right, doctor?"

"Yes, you'll be able to use it again. You were lucky."

I got dressed and out of there. It still felt raw in my shorts. Driving up Vermont I stopped at the grocery. I was out of food. I pushed my cart about picking up hamburger, bread, eggs.

Someday I must tell Bernadette about my close call. If she reads this, she'll know. Last I heard she and Karl went to Florida. She got pregnant. Karl wanted the abortion bit. She didn't. They split. She's still in Florida. She's living with Karl's buddy, Willy. Willy does pornography. He wrote me a couple of weeks ago. I haven't answered yet.

SOME HANGOVER

Kevin's wife handed him the phone. It was Saturday morning. They were still in bed.

"It's Bonnie," she said.

"Hello, Bonnie?"

"You awake, Kevin?"

"Yeah, yeah."

"Listen, Kevin, Jeanjean told me."

"She told you what?"

"That you took her and Cathy into the closet and took their panties off and sniffed their peepees."

"Sniffed their peepees?"

"That's what she said."

"Good God, Bonnie, are you trying to be funny?"

"Jeanjean doesn't lie about such things. She said you took Cathy and her into the closet and took their panties off and sniffed their peepees."

"Now wait a minute, Bonnie!"

"Wait, *hell*! Tom's really mad, he is threatening to kill you. And I think it's awful, unbelievable! Mother thinks I should call my lawyer."

Bonnie hung up. Kevin put the phone down.

"What is it?" asked his wife.

"Now look, Gwen, it's nothing."

"Are you ready for breakfast?"

"I don't think I can eat."

"Kevin, what is the matter?"

"Bonnie claims I took Jeanjean and Cathy into the closet and took their panties off and sniffed their peepees."

"Oh, come on!"

"That's what she said."

"Did you?"

"God, Gwen, I was drinking. Last thing I remember about that party, I was standing out on the front lawn looking at the moon. It was a big moon, I had never seen a bigger moon."

"And you don't remember the other?"

"No."

"You black out when you are drinking, Kevin. You know you black out when you are drinking."

"I don't think I'd do anything like that. I'm no child molester."

"Little girls 8 and 10 years old are pretty cute."

Gwen walked into the bathroom. When she came out she said, "I pray to God it happened. I'd be happy to God if it really happened!"

"What? What the hell are you saying?"

"I mean it. It might slow you down. It might make you think twice about your drinking. It might even make you quit drinking entirely. Every time you go to a party you've got to drink more than anybody, you have got to *pour* it down. Then you always do something foolish and disgusting, although usually in the past it has been with a full-grown woman."

"Gwen, the whole thing has got to be some kind of joke."

"It's no joke. Wait until you have to face Cathy and Jeanjean and Tom and Bonnie!"

"Gwen, I love those two little girls."

"What?"

"Oh shit, forget it."

Gwen walked into the kitchen and Kevin went to the bathroom. He threw cold water on his face and looked at himself in the mirror. What did a child molester look like? Answer: like everybody else until they told him he was one.

Kevin sat down to crap. Crapping seemed so safe, so warm. Surely this thing had not happened. He was in his own bathroom. There was his towel, there was his washrag, there was the toilet paper, there was the bathtub, and under his feet, soft and warm, was the bathroom rug, red, clean, comfortable. Kevin finished, wiped, flushed, washed his hands like a civilized man and walked into the kitchen. Gwen had the bacon on. She poured him a cup of coffee.

"Thanks."

"Scrambled?"

"Scrambled."

"Married ten years and you always say 'scrambled.' "

"More amazing than that, you always ask."

"Kevin, if this gets around, you are out of a job. The bank does not need a branch manager who is a child molester."

"I guess not."

"Kevin, we've got to have a meeting with the families involved. We've got to sit down and talk this thing out."

"You sound like a scene from *The Godfather*."

"Kevin, you're in big trouble. There's no way of getting around it. You're in trouble. Put your toast in. Push it in slow or it will pop right up, there is something wrong with the spring."

Kevin put the toast in. Gwen dished out the bacon and eggs.

"Jeanjean is something of a flirt. She's just like her mother. It's a wonder it hasn't happened before now. Not that I'm saying there is any excuse."

She sat down. The toast came up and Kevin handed her a slice.

"Gwen, when you don't remember something it is very strange. It's the same as if it never happened."

"Some murderers forget what they've done too."

"You're not comparing this to murder?"

"It can seriously affect the future of two little girls."

"A lot of things can."

"I'd have to guess that your behavior was destructive."

"Maybe it was constructive. Maybe they liked it."

"It's been a hell of a long time," Gwen said, "since you sniffed my peepee."

"That's right, bring yourself into it."

"I am in it. We live in a community of 20,000 people and something like this is not going to stay a secret."

"How are they going to prove it? It's two little girls' word against mine."

"More coffee?"

"Yes."

"I meant to get you some tabasco sauce. I know you like it on your eggs."

"You always forget."

"I know. Listen, Kevin, you finish your breakfast. You take as long as you want to eat. Excuse me. I have something to do."

"All right."

He wasn't sure if he loved Gwen but living with her was comfortable. She took care of all the details and details were what drove a man crazy. He put plenty of butter on his toast. Butter was one of man's last luxuries. Automobiles would one day be too expensive to buy and everybody would just sit around eating butter and waiting. The Jesus freaks who talked about the end of the world were looking better every day. Kevin finished his toast and butter and Gwen walked back in.

"All right, it's arranged. I've called everybody."

"What do you mean?"

"There's going to be a meeting in one hour at Tom's place."

"Tom's place?"

"Yes, Tom and Bonnie and Bonnie's parents and Tom's brother and sister—they'll all be there."

"Will the kids be there?"

"No."

"What about Bonnie's lawyer?"

"Are you frightened?"

"Wouldn't you be?"

"I don't know. I have never sniffed a little girl's peepee."

"Why the hell not?"

"Because it is neither decent nor civilized."

"And where has our decent civilization led us?"

"I guess to men like you who take little girls into closets."

"You seem to be enjoying this."

"I don't know if those little girls will ever forgive you."

"You want me to ask their forgiveness? I have to do that? For something I don't even remember?"

"Why not?"

"Let them forget it. Why drive the point home?"

★   ★   ★

As Kevin and Gwen drove up in front of Tom's place, Tom stood up and said, "Here they are. Now we've all got to stay calm. There's a decent, fair way to settle this. We're all mature human beings. We can settle everything among ourselves. There's no need to call the police. Last night I wanted to kill Kevin. Now I just want to help him."

The six relatives of Jeanjean and Cathy sat and waited. The doorbell rang. Tom opened the door. "Hello, folks."

"Hello," said Gwen. Kevin didn't say anything.

"Sit down."

They walked over and sat on the couch. "Drink?"

"No," said Gwen.

"Scotch and soda," said Kevin.

Tom mixed the drink, then handed it to Kevin. Kevin tossed it off, reached in his pocket for a cigarette.

"Kevin," said Tom, "we've decided you should see a psychologist."

"Not a psychiatrist?"

"No, a psychologist."

"All right."

"And we think you should pay for any therapy Jeanjean and Cathy might need."

"All right."

"We're going to keep this quiet, for your sake and for the sake of the children."

"Thanks."

"Kevin, there's only one thing we'd like to know. We're your friends. We've been friends for years. Just one thing. *Why do you drink so much?*"

"Hell, I don't know. I guess, mostly, I just get bored."

A WORKING DAY

Joe Mayer was a freelance writer. He had a hangover and the telephone awakened him at 9 a.m. He got up and answered it. "Hello?"

"Hi, Joe. How's it going?"

"Oh, beautiful."

"Beautiful, eh?"

"Yes?"

"Vicki and I just moved into our new house. We don't have a phone yet. But I can give you the address. You got a pen there?"

"Just a minute."

Joe took down the address.

"I didn't like that last story of yours I saw in *Hot Angel*."

"O.K." said Joe.

"I don't mean I didn't like it, I mean I don't like it compared to most of your stuff. By the way, do you know where Buddy Edwards is? Griff Martin who used to edit *Hot Tales* is looking for him. I thought you might know."

"I don't know where he is."

"I think he might be in Mexico."

"He might be."

"Well, listen, we'll be around to see you soon."

"Sure." Joe hung up. He put a couple of eggs in a pan of water, set some coffee water on and took an Alka Seltzer. Then he went back to bed.

The phone rang again. He got up and answered it.

"Joe?"

"Yes?"

"This is Eddie Greer."

"Oh yes."

"We want you to read for a benefit . . ."

"What is it?"

"For the I.R.A."

"Listen, Eddie, I don't go for politics or religion or whatever. I really don't know what's going on over there. I don't have a tv, read the papers . . . any of that. I don't know who's right or who's wrong, if there is such a thing."

"England's wrong, man."

"I can't read for the I.R.A., Eddie."

"All right, then . . ."

The eggs were done. He sat down, peeled them, put on some toast and mixed the Sanka in with the hot water. He got down the eggs and toast and had two coffees. Then he went back to bed.

He was just about asleep when the phone rang again. He got up and answered it.

"Mr. Mayer?"

"Yes?"

"I'm Mike Haven, I'm a friend of Stuart Irving's. We once appeared in *Stone Mule* together when *Stone Mule* was edited in Salt Lake City."

"Yes?"

"I'm down from Montana for a week. I'm staying at the Hotel Sheraton here in town. I'd like to come see you and talk to you."

"Today's a bad day, Mike."

"Well, maybe I can come over later in the week?"

"Yes, why don't you call me later on?"

"You know, Joe, I write just like you do, both in poetry and prose. I want to bring some of my stuff over and read it to you. You'll be surprised. My stuff is really powerful."

"Oh yes?"

"You'll see."

The mailman was next. One letter. Joe opened it:

Dear Mr. Mayer:
   I got your address from Sylvia who you used to write to in Paris many years ago. Sylvia is still alive in San Fran-

cisco today and still writing her wild and prophetic and angelic and mad poems. I'm living in Los Angeles now and would just love to come and visit you! Please tell me when it would be all right with you.

love, Diane

Joe got out of his robe and got dressed. The phone rang again. He walked over to it, looked at it and didn't answer it. He walked out, got into his car and drove it toward Santa Anita. He drove slowly. He turned the radio on and got some symphony music. It wasn't too smoggy. He drove down Sunset, took his favorite cutoff, drove over the hill toward Chinatown, past the Annex, up past Little Joe's, past Chinatown and took the slow easy ride past the railroad yards, looking down at the old brown boxcars. If he were any damned good at painting he'd like to get that one down. Maybe he'd paint them anyhow. He drove in up Broadway and over Huntington Drive to the track. He got a corned beef sandwich and a coffee, split the Form and sat down. It looked like a fair card.

He caught Rosalena in the first at $10.80, Wife's Objection in the second at $9.20 and hooked them in the daily double for $48.40. He'd had $2 win on Rosalena and $5 win on Wife's Objection, so he was $73.20 up. He ran out on Sweetott, was second with Harbor Point, second with Pitch Out, second with Brannan, all win bets, and he was sitting $48.20 ahead when he hit $20 win on Southern Cream, which brought him back to $73.20 again.

It wasn't bad at the track. He only met three people he knew. Factory workers. Black. From the old days.

The eighth race was the problem. Cougar who was packing 128 was in against Unconscious packing 123. Joe didn't consider the others in the race. He couldn't make up his mind. Cougar was 3-to-5 and Unconscious was 7-to-2. Being $73.20 ahead he felt he could afford the luxury of betting the 3-to-5 shot. He laid $30 win. Cougar broke sluggishly, acting as if he were running in a ditch. By the time he was halfway around the first turn he was 17 lengths back of the lead horse. Joe knew he had a loser. At the finish his 3-to-5 was five lengths back and the race was over.

He went $10 and $10 on Barbizon, Jr. and Lost at Sea in the ninth, failed, and walked out with $23.20. It was easier picking tomatoes. He got into his old car and drove slowly back . . .

★ ★ ★

Just as he got into the tub the doorbell rang. He toweled and got into his shirt and pants. It was Max Billinghouse. Max was in his early twenties, toothless, red-haired. He worked as a janitor and always wore bluejeans and a dirty white t-shirt. He sat down in a chair and crossed his legs

"Well, Mayer, what's happening?"

"What do you mean?"

"I mean, are you surviving on your writing?"

"At the moment."

"Is there anything new?"

"Not since you were here last week."

"How did your poetry reading come out?"

"It was all right."

"The crowd that goes to poetry readings is a very phoney crowd."

"Most crowds are."

"You got any candy?" Max asked.

"Candy?"

"Yeah, I got a sweet tooth. I've got this sweet tooth."

"I don't have any candy."

Max got up and walked into the kitchen. He came out with a tomato and two slices of bread. He sat down.

"Jesus, you don't have anything to eat around here."

"I'm going to have to go to the store."

"You know," said Max, "if I had to read in front of a crowd, I'd really insult them, I'd hurt their feelings."

"You might."

"But I can't write. I think I'm going to carry around a tape recorder. I talk to myself sometimes when I'm working. Then I can write down what I say and I'll have a story."

Max was an hour-and-a-half man. He was good for an hour-and-a-half. He never listened, he just talked. After an hour-and-a-half, Max stood up.

"Well, I gotta go."

"O.K., Max."

Max left. He always talked about the same things. How he had insulted some people on a bus. How once he had met Charles Manson. How a man was better off with a whore than with a decent woman. Sex was in the head. He didn't need new clothes, a new car. He was a loner. He didn't need people.

Joe went into the kitchen and found a can of tuna and made three sandwiches. He took out the pint of scotch he had been saving and poured a good scotch and water. He flicked the radio to the classical station. "The Blue Danube Waltz." He flicked it off. He finished the sandwiches. The doorbell rang. Joe walked to the door and opened it. It was Hymie. Hymie had a soft job somewhere in some city government near L.A. He was a poet.

"Listen," he said, "that book I had an idea for, *An Anthology of L.A. Poets*, let's forget it."

"All right."

Hymie sat down. "We need a new title. I think I have it. *Mercy for the Warmongers*. Think about it."

"I kind of like it," said Joe.

"And we can say, 'This book is for Franco, and for Lee Harvey Oswald and Adolf Hitler.' Now I'm Jewish, so that takes some guts. What do you think?"

"Sounds good."

Hymie got up and did his imitation of a typical old-time Jewish fat man, a very Jewish fat man. He spit on himself and sat down. Hymie was very funny. Hymie was the funniest man Joe knew. Hymie was good for an hour. After an hour, Hymie stood up and left. He always talked about the same things. How most of the poets were very bad. That it was tragic, it was so tragic it was laughable. What could a guy do?

Joe had another good scotch and water and walked over to the typewriter. He typed two lines, then the phone rang. It was Dunning at the hospital. Dunning liked to drink a lot of beer. He'd done his 20 in the army. Dunning's father had been the editor of a famous little magazine. Dunning's father had died in June. Dunning's wife was ambitious. She had pushed him to be a doctor, hard. He'd made it to chiropractor. And was working as a male nurse while trying to save up for an eight or ten thousand dollar x-ray machine.

"How about coming over and drinking some beer with you?" asked Dunning.

"Listen, can we put it off?" asked Joe.

"What'sa matter? You writing?"

"Just started."

"All right. I'll take a rain check."

"Thanks, Dunning."

Joe sat down at the machine again. It wasn't bad. He got halfway down the page when he heard footsteps. Then a knock. Joe opened the door.

It was two young kids. One with a black beard, the other smooth-shaven.

The kid with the beard said, "I saw you at your last reading."

"Come in," said Joe.

They came in. They had six bottles of imported beer, green bottles.

"I'll get an opener," said Joe.

They sat there sucking at the beer.

"It was a good reading," said the kid with the beard.

"Who was your major influence?" asked the one without the beard.

"Jeffers. Longer poems. *Tamar. Roan Stallion.* So forth."

"Any new writing that interests you?"

"No."

"They say you're coming out of the underground, that you're part of the Establishment. What do you think of that?"

"Nothing."

There were some more questions of the same order. The boys were only good for one beer apiece. Joe took care of the other four. They left in 45 minutes. But the one without the beard said, just as they left, "We'll be back."

Joe sat down to the machine again with a new drink. He couldn't type. He got up and walked to the phone. He dialed. And waited. She was there. She answered.

"Listen," said Joe, "let me get out of here. Let me come down there and lay up."

"You mean you want to stay tonight?"

"Yes."

"Again?"

"Yes, again."

"All right."

Joe walked around the corner of the porch and right down the driveway. She lived three or four courts down. He knocked. Lu let him in. The lights were out. She just had on panties and led him to the bed.

"God," he moaned.

"What is it?"

"Well, it's all unexplainable in a way or *almost* unexplainable."

"Just take off your clothes and come to bed."

Joe did. He crawled in. He didn't know at first if it would work again. So many nights in a row. But her body was there and it was a young body. And the lips were open and real. Joe floated in. It was good being in the dark. He worked her over good. He even got down there again and tongued that cunt. Then as he mounted, after four or five strokes he heard a voice . . .

"Mayer . . . I'm looking for a Joe Mayer . . ."

He heard his landlord's voice. His landlord was drunk.

"Well, if he ain't in that front apartment, you check this one back here. He's either in one or the other."

Joe got in four or five more strokes before the knocking began at the door. Joe slid out and, naked, went to the door. He opened a side window.

"Yeah?"

"Hey, Joe! Hi, Joe, what you doin' Joe?"

"Nothing."

"Well, how about some beer, Joe?"

"No," said Joe. He slammed the side window and walked back to the bed, got in.

"Who was it?" she asked.

"I don't know. I didn't recognize the face."

"Kiss me, Joe. Just don't lay there."

He kissed her as the Southern California moon came through the Southern California curtains. He was Joe Mayer. Freelance writer.

He had it made.

THE MAN WHO LOVED ELEVATORS

Harry stood in the apartment house driveway waiting for the elevator to come down. Just as the door opened he heard a woman's voice behind him. "Just a moment, please!" She stepped into the elevator and the door closed. She had on a yellow dress, her hair was piled on top of her head, and goofy pearl earrings swung on long silver chains. She had a large ass and was heavily built. Her breasts and body seemed to be striving to burst out of that yellow dress. Her eyes were the palest green and looked right through him. She carried a bag of groceries with the word *Vons* printed on it. Her lips were smeared with lipstick. Her thick painted lips were obscene, almost ugly, an insult. The bright red lipstick glistened and Harry reached over and pushed the EMERGENCY button.

It worked, the elevator stopped. Harry moved toward her. With one hand he lifted her skirt and stared at her legs. She had unbelievable legs, all muscle and flesh. She seemed stricken, frozen. He grabbed her as she dropped the bag of groceries. Cans of vegetables, an avocado, toilet paper, packaged meat and three candy bars spilled to the elevator floor. Then his mouth was on those lips. They opened. He reached down and lifted the skirt. He kept his mouth on hers and worked the panties off. Then, standing up, he took her, banging her hard against the elevator wall. When he finished, he zipped up, hit the third floor button, and waited, his back to her. When the door opened, he stepped out. The door closed behind him and the elevator was gone.

* * *

Harry walked down to his apartment, put the key in and opened the door. His wife, Rochelle, was in the kitchen cooking dinner.

"How'd it go?" she asked.

"Same old shit," he said.

"Dinner in ten minutes," she said.

Harry walked to the bathroom, got out of his things and took a shower. The job was getting to him. Six years and he didn't have a dime in the bank. That's how they hooked you—they gave you just enough to keep alive but they never gave you enough so you could finally escape.

He soaped up good, washed off and stood there, letting the very hot water run down the back of his neck. It took away the fatigue. He toweled off and put on his robe, walked into the kitchen and sat down at the table. Rochelle was dishing it out. Meatballs and gravy. She made good meatballs and gravy.

"Listen," he said, "give me some good news."

"Good news?"

"You know what."

"The period?"

"Yes."

"I haven't had it."

"Christ."

"The coffee's not ready."

"You always forget."

"I know. I don't know what makes me do that."

Rochelle sat down and they began eating without the coffee. The meatballs were good.

"Harry," she said, "we can get an abortion."

"All right," he said. "If it comes to that, we'll do it."

The next evening he got on the elevator and rode alone. He rode to the third floor and got out. Then he turned around, got back in and pushed the button again. He rode down to the driveway, got out, walked over to his car and sat and waited. He saw her coming up the driveway, this time without any groceries. He opened his car door.

This time she had on a red dress, shorter and tighter-fitting than the yellow one. Her hair was down and it was long. It almost reached her behind. She had on the same goofy earrings and her lips were more heavily smeared with lipstick than before. As she stepped into the elevator he followed her. They rose up and once again he pushed the EMERGENCY button. Then he was upon her, his lips on that red obscene mouth. Again she didn't have on pantyhose, just red knee stockings. Harry worked the panties off and put it in. They banged against all four walls. It lasted longer this time. Then Harry zipped up, turned his back on her and pushed the "3" button.

When he opened the door Rochelle was singing. She had a terrible voice so Harry got into the shower in a hurry. He came out in his robe, sat at the table.

"Christ," he said, "they laid off four guys today, even Jim Bronson."

"That's too bad," said Rochelle.

There were steaks and french fries, salad and hot garlic bread. Not bad.

"You know how long Jim's been there?"

"No."

"Five years."

Rochelle didn't answer. "Five years," said Harry. "They just don't care, those bastards have no mercy."

"I didn't forget the coffee this time, Harry."

She leaned over and kissed him as she poured his cup. "I'm improving, you see?"

"Yeah."

She went and sat down. "My period started today."

"What? Is it true?"

"Yes, Harry."

"That's great, great . . ."

"I don't want a kid until you want one, Harry."

"Rochelle, we ought to *celebrate!* A bottle of good wine! I'll go get one after dinner."

"I've already got it, Harry."

Harry got up and walked around the table. He stood almost behind Rochelle and tilted her head backwards with one hand under her chin and kissed her. "I love you, baby."

They ate dinner. It was a good dinner. And a good bottle of wine . . .

★   ★   ★

Harry got out of his car as she walked up the driveway. She waited for him and they got on the elevator together. She had on a blue and white dress, a flower print, white shoes, white ankle socks. Her hair was piled up on her head again and she smoked a Benson and Hedges cigarette.

Harry pushed the EMERGENCY button.

"Wait a minute, mister!"

It was the second time Harry had heard her voice. The voice was a bit hoarse but it wasn't a bad voice at all.

"Yes," asked Harry, "what is it?"

"Let's go to my apartment."

"All right."

She pushed the "4" button, they went up, the door opened and they walked down the hall to 404. She unlocked the door.

"Nice place," said Harry.

"I like it. Can I get you something to drink?"

"Sure."

She walked into the kitchen. "I'm Nana," she said.

"I'm Harry."

"I know you are but what's your name?"

"You're funny," said Harry.

She came out with two drinks and they sat on the couch and drank them. "I work at Zody's discount," said Nana. "I'm a counter girl at Zody's."

"That's nice."

"What the hell's nice about it?"

"I mean, it's nice that we're here together."

"Really?"

"Sure."

"Let's go into the bedroom."

Harry followed her. Nana finished her drink and set the empty glass on the dresser. She walked into the closet. It was a large closet. She began to sing and to remove her clothing. Nana sang better than Rochelle. Harry sat on the edge of the bed and finished his drink. Nana came out of the closet and stretched out on the bed. She was naked. The hair on her cunt was much darker than the hair on her head.

"Well?" she said.

"Oh," said Harry. He took off his shoes, he took off his stock-

110

ings, he took off his shirt, his pants, his undershirt, his shorts. Then he got on the bed beside her. She turned her head and he kissed her. "Listen," he said, "do we have to have all these lights on?"

"Of course not." Nana got up and switched off the overhead light and the bedside lamp. Harry felt her mouth on his. Her tongue entered, flicked in and out. Harry climbed on top of her. She was very soft, something like a waterbed. He kissed and licked her breasts, kissed her mouth and her neck. He continued to kiss her for some time.

"What's the matter?" she asked.

"I don't know," he said.

"It's not working, is it?"

"No."

Harry got off and began dressing in the dark. Nana switched on the bed lamp.

"What are you? An elevator freak?"

"No, no . . ."

"You can only do it in elevators, is that it?"

"No, no, you were the first one, really. I don't know what came over me."

"But I'm here now," Nana said.

"I know it," he said, pulling his pants on. Then he sat down and started putting on his shoes and stockings.

"Listen, you son of a bitch—"

"Yes?"

"When you are ready and you want me, come to my apartment, understand?"

"Yes, I understand."

Harry was fully dressed and standing again.

"No more on the elevator, understand?"

"I understand."

"If you ever rape me on the elevator again I'll call the law, that's a promise."

"O.K., O.K."

Harry walked out of the bedroom, through the living room and out the apartment door. He walked down to the elevator and pushed the button. The door opened and he stepped in. The elevator began to descend. There was a petite Oriental woman standing next to him. She had black hair. Black skirt, white blouse, pantyhose, tiny feet, high-heeled shoes. She was dark complexioned, with just a trace of lipstick. That very small body had an amazing, sexy behind. The eyes were brown and very deep and looked tired. Harry reached and pushed the EMERGENCY button. As he moved toward her she screamed. He slapped her hard across the face, got out his handkerchief and forced it into her mouth. He locked one of his arms about her waist and as she clawed him across the face with her free hand he reached down and pulled up her skirt. He liked what he saw.

HEAD JOB

Margie usually began playing Chopin nocturnes when the sun went down. She lived in a large house set back from the street and by sundown she was high on brandy or scotch. At 43 her figure was still slim, her face delicate. Her husband had died young five years before and she lived in apparent solitude. The husband had been a doctor and lucky in the stock market and the money was invested to give her a fixed income of $2,000 a month. A good portion of the $2,000 went for brandy or scotch.

She'd had two lovers since the death of her husband but both affairs had been desultory and short-lived. Men seemed to lack magic, most of them were bad lovers, sexually and spiritually. Their interests seemed to center on new cars, sports and television. At least Harry, her late husband, had taken her to an occasional symphony. God knows, Mehta was a very bad conductor but he beat watching Laverne and Shirley. Margie had simply resigned herself to an existence without the male animal. She lived a quiet life with her piano and her brandy and her scotch. And when the sun went down she needed her piano very much, and her Chopin, and her scotch and/or brandy. She would begin to light one cigarette after another as the evening arrived.

Margie had one amusement. A new couple had moved into the house next door. Only they were hardly a couple. He was 20 years older than the woman, was bearded, powerful, violent and appeared half-mad. He was an ugly man who always looked either intoxicated or hung over. The woman he lived with was odd, too—sullen, indifferent. Almost in a dream-state. The two appeared to have an affinity for each other, yet it was as if two enemies had been thrown together. They fought continually. Margie usually would first hear the woman's voice, then suddenly and loudly she would hear the man's, and the man always screamed some vile indecency. Sometimes the voices would be followed by the sound of breaking glass. More often, though, the man would be seen driving away in his old car and the neighborhood would be quiet for two or three days until his return. Twice the police had taken the man away, but he always returned.

One day Margie saw his photo in the newspaper—the man was the poet Marx Renoffski. She had heard of his work. She went to the bookstore the next day and bought all his available books. That afternoon she mixed his poetry with her brandy and as it got dark that night she forgot to play her Chopin nocturnes. She gathered from some of the love poems that he was living with the sculptress, Karen Reeves. For some reason, Margie didn't feel as lonely as she once had.

The house belonged to Karen and there were many parties. Always during the parties, when the music and the laughter were the loudest, she would see the large, bearded figure of Marx Renoffski emerge from the rear of the house. He would sit in the backyard alone with his beer bottle in the moonlight. It was then that Margie would remember his love poems and wish she could meet him.

Friday night, several weeks after she had bought his books, she heard them arguing loudly. Marx had been drinking and Karen's voice became more and more shrill. "Listen," she heard Marx's voice, "any time I want a goddamned drink I'm gonna take a goddamned drink!" "You're the ugliest thing that has ever happened in my life!" she heard Karen say. Then there were sounds of a scuffle. Margie turned out the lights and pressed close to the window. "God damn you," she heard Marx say, "you keep attacking me and I'll let you have one!"

She saw Marx come out on the front porch carrying his typewriter. It wasn't a portable, but a standard model, and Marx staggered down the steps carrying it, almost falling several times. "I'm getting rid of your head," Karen screamed. "I'm throwing your head out!" "Go ahead," Marx said, "dump it." She saw Marx load the typewriter into his car and then she saw a large heavy object, evidently the head, come flying off the end of the porch and into her yard. It bounced and settled just under a large rose bush. Marx drove off in his car. All the lights went out in Karen Reeves' house and it was quiet.

When Margie awakened the next morning it was 8:45. She made her toilet, put two eggs on to boil, and had a coffee with a jigger of brandy. She walked to the front window. The large clay object was still under the rose bush. She went back, took out the eggs, cooled them under cold water and peeled them. She sat down to eat the eggs and opened a copy of Marx Renoffski's latest book of poems, *One, Two, Three, I Love Me.* She opened it near the middle:

> oh, I've got squadrons
> of pain
> battalions, armies of
> pain
> continents of pain
> ha, ha, ha,
> and
> I've got you.

Margie finished the eggs, put two jiggers of brandy in her second coffee, drank it, put on her green striped pants, her yellow sweater, and looking a little bit like Katharine Hepburn looked at 43, she slipped into her red sandals and walked out into her front yard. Marx's car wasn't there on the street and Karen's house looked very quiet. She walked toward the rose bush. The sculpted head was face-down under the bush. Margie could feel her heart beat. She took her foot and rolled the head over and the face looked up at her out of the dirt. It certainly was Marx Renoffski. She picked Marx up, and holding him carefully against her pale yellow sweater she carried him into the house. She put him on top of her piano, then had a brandy and water and sat down and looked at him while she drank it. Marx was craggy and ugly but very real. Karen Reeves was a good sculptress. Margie was thankful to Karen Reeves. She continued to study Marx's head, she could see everything there: kindness, hatred, fear, madness, love, humor, but she saw mostly the love and the humor. When KSUK came on the air with the classical music program at noon, she turned the radio on loudly and began to drink with real enjoyment.

Around 4 p.m., still drinking brandy, she began talking to him. "Marx, I understand you. I could bring you real happiness."

Marx didn't answer, he just sat there on top of the piano. "Marx, I've read your books. You're a sensitive and gifted man, Marx, and so funny. I understand you darling, I'm not like that . . . that other woman."

Marx just kept grinning, looking at her through his little slitted eyes.

"Marx, I could play you Chopin . . . the nocturnes, the études."

Margie sat down at the piano and began playing. He was right there. One just *knew* that Marx never watched football on tv. He probably watched Shakespeare and Ibsen and Chekov on Channel 28. And like in his poems, he was a great lover. She poured more brandy and played on. Marx Renoffski listened.

When Margie was finished with her concert, she looked at Marx. He had enjoyed it. She was sure of it. She stood up. Marx's head was just level with hers. She bent over and gave him a little kiss. She drew back. He was grinning, he was grinning his delightful grin. She put her mouth on his again and gave him a slow, passionate kiss.

The next morning Marx was still there on the piano. Marx Renoffski, poet, modern poet, alive, dangerous, lovely and sensitive. She looked out the front window. Marx's car was not there yet. He was staying away. He was staying away from that . . . bitch.

Margie turned and spoke to him. "Marx, you need a good woman." She walked to the kitchen, put two eggs on to boil, put a jigger of scotch into her coffee. She hummed to herself. The day was identical to the preceding one. Only better. It felt better. She read some more of Marx's work. She even wrote a poem of her own:

> this most divine accident
> has brought us
>   together
> even though you are clay
> and I am flesh
> we have touched
> we have somehow touched

At 4 p.m. the doorbell rang. She walked to the door and opened it. It was Marx Renoffski. He was intoxicated.

"Baby," he said, "we know you got the head. What are you going to do with my head?"

Margie couldn't answer. Marx pushed his way in.

"All right, where is the goddamned thing? Karen wants it back."

The head was in the music room. Marx walked around. "Nice place you got here. You live alone, don't you?"

"Yes."

"What's the matter, you afraid of men?"

"No."

"Listen, next time Karen runs me out I think I'll come over here. O.K.?"

Margie didn't answer.

"You didn't answer. That means O.K. Well, fine. But I still have to get that head. Listen. I hear you playing Chopin when the sun goes down. You got class. I like class broads. I'll bet you drink brandy, don't you?"

"Yes."

"Pour me a brandy. Three jiggers in a half glass of water."

Margie went into the kitchen. When she came out with the drink he was in the music room. He'd found the head. He was leaning against it, his elbow resting on top of the skull. She handed him his drink.

"Thanks. Yeah, class, you're class. You paint, write, compose? You do anything besides play Chopin?"

"No."

"Ah," he said, raising his drink and downing half of it. "I bet you do."

"Do what?"

"Fuck. I bet you're a great fuck."

"I don't know."

"Well, I know. And you shouldn't waste it. I don't want to see you waste it."

Marx Renoffski finished his drink and placed it on top of the piano next to the head. He walked over to her and grabbed her. He smelled of vomit, cheap wine and bacon. Needle-like hairs from his beard poked into her face as he kissed her. Then he pulled his face away and looked at her with his tiny eyes. "You don't wanna miss out on life, baby!" She felt his penis rise against her. "I eat pussy too. I never ate pussy until I was 50. Karen taught me. Now I'm the best in the world."

"I don't like to be rushed," Margie said weakly.

"Ah, that's fine! That's what I like: *spirit!* Chaplin fell in love with Goddard when he saw her biting into an apple! I'll bet you bite an apple damn good! I'll bet you can do other things with your mouth, yes, yes!"

Then he kissed her again. When he broke away he asked Margie, "Where's the bedroom?"

"Why?"

"Why? Because that's where we're going to do it!"

"Do what?"

"Fuck, of course!"

"Get out of my house!"

"You don't mean it?"

"I mean it."

"You mean you don't want to fuck?"

"Exactly."

"Listen, there are ten thousand women who want to go to bed with me!"

"I'm not one of them."

"O.K., pour me another drink and I'll go."

"It's a bargain." Margie went to the kitchen, put three jiggers of brandy into a half glass of water, came out and handed it to him.

"Listen, do you know who I am?"

"Yes."

"I'm Marx Renoffski, the poet."

"I said I knew who you were."

"Oh," said Marx, and he drained the glass. "Well, I gotta go. Karen, she don't trust me."

"You tell Karen that I think she's a fine sculptress."

"Oh, yeah, sure . . ." Marx picked up the head, walked through the room and toward the door. Margie followed him. Marx stopped at the door. "Listen, don't you ever get hot pants?"

"Of course."

"What do you do?"

"I masturbate."

Marx drew himself up. "Madam, that's a crime against nature and, more importantly, against me." He closed the door. She

118

watched him go carefully down the walk carrying his head. Then he turned and went up the path to Karen Reeves' house.

Margie went into the music room. She sat down at the piano. The sun was going down. She was right on schedule. She began to play Chopin. She played Chopin better than she ever had before.

TURKEYNECK MORNING

At 6 a.m. Barney awakened and began poking her in the ass with his cock. Shirley pretended to be asleep. Barney poked harder and harder. She got up out of bed and went to the bathroom and urinated. When she came out he had the quilt off and was poking it up in the air under the bedsheet.

"Look, baby!" he said. "Mt. Everest!"

"Should I start breakfast?"

"Breakfast, shit! Come on back in here!"

Shirley got back in and he grabbed her head and kissed her. His breath was bad and his beard was worse. He took her hand and placed it on his cock.

"Think of all the women who'd like to have this thing!"

"Barney, I'm just not in the mood."

"What do you mean, you're not in the mood?"

"I mean, I just don't feel sexy."

"You will, baby, you will!"

They slept without pajamas in the summer and he climbed on top of her. "Open up, goddamn it! You sick?"

"Barney, please . . ."

"Please, what? I want some ass and I'm going to get some ass!"

He kept forcing with his cock until he entered her. "You god-damned whore, I'll rip you wide open!"

Barney fucked like a machine. She had no feelings for him. How could any woman marry a man like that? she wondered. How could any woman live with a man like that for three years? When they had first met he hadn't seemed so . . . much like hardwood.

"You like that turkeyneck, kid?"

The full weight of his heavy body was on her. He was sweating. He offered her no relief.

"I'm coming, baby, I'm COMING!"

Barney rolled off and wiped on the sheet. Shirley got up, went to the bathroom and douched. Then she went to the kitchen to prepare breakfast. She put on the potatoes, the bacon, the coffee. She broke the eggs into the bowl and scrambled them. She had on her slippers and her bathrobe. The bathrobe said, "HERS." Barney came out of the bathroom. He had shaving cream on his face.

"Hey, baby, where are those green shorts of mine with the red stripes?"

She didn't answer.

"Listen, I asked you where those shorts were!"

"I don't know."

"You don't know? I bust my hump out there from eight to twelve hours a day and you don't know where my shorts are?"

"I don't know."

"The coffee's boiling over! *Look!*"

Shirley shut the flame off.

"Either you don't make coffee at all, either you forget the coffee or you boil it all away! Or you forget to buy bacon or you burn the fucking toast or you lose my shorts, or you do *some* fucking thing. You always do *some* fucking thing!"

"Barney, I'm not feeling good . . ."

"And you're *always* not feeling good! When the *hell* you gonna *start* feeling good? I go out and bust my hump and you lay around reading magazines all day and feeling sorry for your soft ass. You think it's *easy* out there? You realize there are ten percent unemployed? You realize I've got to fight for my job every day, day after day while you sit in an armchair feeling sorry for yourself? And drinking wine and smoking cigarettes and talking to your friends? Girlfriends, boyfriends, whoever the hell friends. You think it's *easy* for me out there?"

"I know it's not easy, Barney."

"You don't even want to give me a piece of ass anymore."

Shirley poured the scrambled eggs into the pan. "Why don't you finish shaving? Breakfast will be ready soon."

"I mean, what's your reluctance about giving me a piece of ass? That thing rimmed in gold?"

She stirred up the eggs with a fork. Then she picked up the spatula. "It's because I can't stand you anymore, Barney. I hate you."

"You hate me? What do you mean?"

"I mean, I can't stand the way you walk. I can't stand the hairs that stick out of your nose. I don't like your voice, your eyes. I don't like your mind or the way you talk. I don't like you."

"And what about *you?* What do *you* have to offer? *Look* at you! You couldn't get a job in a third-rate whorehouse!"

"I've got one."

He hit her then, open-handed, on the side of the face. She dropped the spatula, lost her balance, hit the side of the sink and caught herself. She picked up the spatula, washed it in the sink, came back and turned the eggs over.

"I don't want breakfast," Barney said.

Shirley turned off all the burners and went back to the bedroom, went to bed. She heard him getting himself ready in the bathroom. She even hated the way he splashed water in the basin while he shaved. And when she heard the electric toothbrush the thought of the bristles in his mouth cleaning his teeth and his gums sickened her. Then there was the sound of hairspray. There was silence. Then the toilet flushed.

He came out. She heard him choosing a shirt from the closet. She heard his keys and his change rattle as he put on his pants. Then she felt the bed give way as he sat on the edge, putting on his stockings and his shoes. Then the bed rose as he stood up. She lay on her stomach, face down, eyes closed. She sensed him looking at her.

"Listen," he said, "I just want to tell you one thing: if it's another man, I'm going to kill you. Got it?"

Shirley didn't answer. Then she felt his fingers around the back of her neck. He bounced her head hard up and down into the pillow. "*Answer me!* Got it? Got it? *You got it?*"

"Yes," she said, "I've got it."

He let go of her. He walked out of the bedroom and into the front room. She heard the door close, then heard him walk down the steps. The car was in the driveway, and she listened to it start. Then she heard the sound of it driving away. Then there was silence.

123

IN AND OUT AND OVER

The problem with an 11 a.m. arrival and an 8 p.m. poetry reading is that it sometimes reduces a man to something they lead on stage only to be looked at, jibed at, knocked down, which is what they want—not enlightenment, but entertainment.

Professor Kragmatz met me at the airport, I met his two dogs in the car, and I met Pulholtz (who had been reading my work for years) and two young students—one a karate expert and the other with a broken leg—back at Howard's house. (Howard was the professor who had issued the invitation for me to read.)

I sat glum and pious, drinking beer, and then almost everyone but Howard had a class to go to. Doors slammed and the dogs barked and left and the clouds darkened and Howard and I and his wife and a young male student sat around. Jacqueline, Howie's wife, played chess with the student.

"I got a new supply," said Howard. He opened his hand on a palm-full of pills. "No. It's my stomach," I said. "Bad shape lately."

At 8 p.m. I got up there. "He's drunk, he's drunk," I could hear the voices from the audience. I had my vodka and orange juice. I gave them an opening swallow to stir up their distaste. I read for an hour.

The applause was fair enough. A young boy came up, trembling. "Mr. Chinaski, I have got to tell you this: you are a beautiful man!" I shook his hand. "It's all right, kid, just keep buying my books." A few had some of my books and I made drawings in them. It was over. I had hustled my ass.

The post-reading party was the same as always, professors and students, bland and dim. Professor Kragmatz got me in the breakfast nook, began asking questions as the groupies slithered about. No, I told him, no, well, yes, parts of T. S. Eliot *were* good. We were too rough on Eliot. Pound, yes, well, we were finding out that Pound was not quite what we thought. No, I couldn't think of any outstanding contemporary American poets, sorry. Concrete poetry? Well, yes, concrete poetry was just like concrete anything else. What, Céline? An old crank with withered testicles. Only one good book, the first one. What? Yes, of course, it's enough. I mean, you haven't written even one have you? Why do I pick on Creeley? I don't anymore. Creeley's built a body of work, that's more than most of his critics have done. Yes, I drink, doesn't everybody? How the hell you going to make it otherwise? Women? Oh yes, women, oh yes, of course. You can't write about fireplugs and empty India ink bottles. Yes, I know about the red wheelbarrow in the rain. Look, Kragmatz, I don't want you to hog me entirely. I better move around . . .

I stayed and slept in the bottom half of a bunk bed under the boy who was the karate expert. I awakened him about 6 a.m. by scratching my hemorrhoids. A stink arose and the female dog who had slept with me all night began nuzzling. I turned on my back and went to sleep again.

When I awakened everybody was gone but Howie. I got up, took a bath, dressed, walked out to see him. He was very sick.

"My god, you're resilient," he said. "You've got the body of a 20-year-old."

"No speed, no bennies, very little hard stuff last night . . . only beer and grass. I lucked it," I told him.

I suggested some soft-boiled eggs. Howard put them on. It began to get dark. It seemed like midnight. Jacqueline phoned and said there was a tornado approaching from the north. It began hailing. We ate our eggs.

Then the poet for the next night's reading arrived with his girl friend and Kragmatz. Howard ran out into the yard and vomited up his eggs. The new poet, Blanding Edwards, began talking. He meant well. He talked about Ginsberg, Corso, Kerouac. Then Blanding Edwards and his girlfriend, Betty (who also wrote poetry), began talking to each other in rapid French.

It got darker, there was lightning, more hail, and the wind, the wind was awful. The beer came out. Kragmatz reminded Edwards to be careful, he had to read that night. Howard got onto his bicycle and pedaled off in the storm to go teach freshman English at the university. Jacqueline arrived. "Where's Howie?"

"He took his two wheels out into the tornado," I said.

"Is he all right?"

"He looked like a 17-year-old boy when he left. He took a couple of aspirin."

The remainder of the afternoon was waiting and trying to avoid literary talk. I got a ride to the airport. I had my $500 check and my satchel of poems. I told them to stay in the car and that someday I would send all of them a picture postcard.

I walked into the waiting room and I heard one guy say to another, "Look at *that* guy!" The natives all had the same hairstyle, the same buckles on their high-heeled shoes, lightweight overcoats, single-breasted suits with brass buttons, striped shirts, neckties that ran the gamut from gold to green. Even their faces were alike: the noses and ears and mouths and expressions were alike. Shallow lakes coated with thin ice. Our plane was late. I stood behind a coffee machine, drank two dark coffees and ate some crackers. Then I went out and stood in the rain.

We left after an hour and a half. The plane rocked and bucked. There was no *New Yorker* magazine. I asked the stewardess for a drink. She said there wasn't any ice. The pilot told us there would be a delay landing in Chicago. They couldn't get clearance. He was a man of truth. We reached Chicago and there was the airport and we circled and circled and circled and I said, "Well, I guess there's nothing to do." I ordered my third drink. The others began to get into the swing of it. Especially after both engines sputtered out at once. They started again and somebody laughed. We drank and we drank and we drank. After we were potted out of our lighttowers they told us they were going to land.

O'Hare again. The thin ice broke. People hustled about, asking obvious questions and getting obvious answers. I saw my flight had no departure time listed. It was 8:30 p.m. I phoned Ann. She said she'd keep calling L.A. International for the arrival time. She asked me how the reading had gone. I told her that it was very hard to fool a college poetry audience. I had only fooled about half of them. "Fine," she said. "Never trust a man who wears a jump suit," I told her.

I stood looking at the legs of a Japanese woman for 15 minutes. Then I found a bar. There was a black man in there dressed in a red leather outfit with a fur collar. They were giving it to him, laughing as if he was a bug crawling on the bar. They did it very well. It took centuries of practice. The black man was trying to be cool, but his back was rigid.

When I went to check the flight board again one-third of the airport was drunk. Hairstyles were coming undone. One man was walking backwards, very drunk, trying to fall on the back of his head and get himself a skull fracture. We all lit cigarettes and waited, watching, hoping he would give his head a damned good whack. I wondered which one of us would get his wallet. I watched him fall, then the horde swooped in to strip him. He was too far away to do me any good. I went back to the bar. The black man was gone. Two guys to my left were arguing. One of them turned to me. "What do you think of war?"

"There's nothing wrong with war," I said.

"Oh, yeah? Yeah?"

"Yeah. When you get into a taxi, that's war. When you buy a loaf of bread, that's war. When you buy a whore, that's war. Sometimes I need bread, taxis and whores."

"Hey, you guys," said the man, "here's a guy who *likes* war."

Another guy came down from the end of the bar. He was dressed like the others. "You like war?"

"There's nothing wrong with it; it's a natural extension of our society."

"How many years you been in?"

"None."

"Where you from?"

"L.A."

"Well, I lost my best buddy to a land mine. BAM! And he was gone."

"But for the grace of God it might have been you."

"Don't get funny."

"I've been drinking. Got a light?"

He put the lighter to the end of my cigarette with obvious distaste. Then he went back down to the end of the bar.

We left on the 7:15 at 11:15. We flew through the air. The poetry hustle was winding down. I'd hit Santa Anita on Friday and score a hundred, get back to the novel. The New York Philharmonic was featuring Ives on Sunday. There was a chance. I ordered another drink.

The lights went out. Nobody could sleep, but they all pretended. I didn't bother. I had a window seat and stared out at the wing and the lights below. Everything was arranged down there in nice straight lines. Ant nests.

We floated into L.A. International. Ann, I love you. I hope my car starts. I hope the sink isn't plugged up. I'm glad I didn't fuck a groupie. I'm glad I'm not very good at getting into bed with strange females. I'm glad I'm an idiot. I'm glad I don't know anything. I'm glad I haven't been murdered. When I look at my hands and they are still on my wrists, I think to myself, I am lucky.

I climbed out of the plane dragging my father's overcoat and my stash of poems. Ann came up to me. I saw her face and I thought, shit, I love her. What am I going to do? The best I could do was to act indifferent, then proceed with her to the parking lot. You must never let them know that you care or they will kill you. I leaned over, pecked her on the cheek. "Damned nice of you to come." "It's all right," she said.

We drove out of L.A. International. I'd done my dirty gig. The poetry hustle. I never solicited. They wanted their whore: they had him. "Kid," I told her, "I sure missed your ass." "I'm hungry," said Ann.

We got to the Chicano place at Alvarado and Sunset. We had green chili burritos. It was over. I still had a woman, a woman I cared for. Such magic is not to be taken casually. I looked at her hair and her face as we drove back home. I stole glances at her when I felt she was not looking.

"How'd the reading go?" she asked.

"The reading went all right," I said.

We drove north up Alvarado. Then to Glendale Boulevard. Everything was good. What I hated was that someday everything would dwindle to zero, the loves, the poems, the gladiolas. Finally we'd be stuffed with dirt like a cheap taco.

Ann pulled into the driveway. We got up, went up the steps,

opened the door and the dog leaped all over us. The moon stood up, the house smelled of lint and roses, the dog leaped upon me. I pulled his ears, punched him in the belly, his eyes opened wide and he grinned.

I LOVE YOU, ALBERT

Louie was sitting in the Red Peacock with a hangover. When the bartender brought him his drink he said, "There's only one other person I've seen in this town who's as crazy as you are." "Yeh?" said Louie, "that's nice. That's damned nice." "And she's here right now," continued the barkeep. "Yeh?" said Louie. "She's the one down there in the blue dress with the beautiful body. But nobody will go near her because she's crazy." "Yeh?" said Louie.

Louie picked up his drink and walked over and sat on the stool next to the girl. "Hello," said Louie. "Hello," she said. Then they sat there side by side for quite a while without saying another word to each other.

Myra (that was her name) suddenly reached behind the bar and came up with a full mix bottle. She raised it over her head and made as if to throw it into the mirror behind the bar. Louie grabbed her arm and said, "No, no, no, no, my dear!" After that the bartender suggested that Myra leave and when she did Louie left with her.

Myra and Louie picked up three fifths of cheap whiskey and got on the bus going to Louie's place, The Delsey Arms Apartments. Myra took off one of her shoes (high-heeled) and attempted to murder the bus driver. Louie restrained Myra with one arm and clutched the three fifths of whiskey with the other. They got off the bus and walked toward Louie's place.

They got in the elevator and Myra began pressing the buttons. The elevator went up, it went down, it went up, it stopped, and Myra kept asking, "Where do you live?" And Louie kept repeating, "Fourth floor, apartment number four."

Myra kept pushing buttons while the elevator went up and down. "Listen," she finally said, "we've been on this thing for years. I'm sorry but I've got to piss." "O.K.," said Louie, "let's make a deal. You let me work the buttons and I'll let you piss."

"Done," she said, and she pulled her panties down, squatted and did the deed. As he watched it trickle across the floor Louie punched the "4" button. They arrived. By then Myra had straightened, pulled up her panties, and was ready to exit.

They went inside Louie's place and began opening bottles. Myra was best at that. They sat facing each other across 10 or 12 feet of space. Louie sat in the chair by the window and Myra sat on the couch. Myra had a fifth and Louie had a fifth and they began.

Fifteen or 20 minutes passed and then Myra noticed some empty bottles on the floor near the couch. She began picking them up, squinting her eyes and throwing the empty bottles at Louie's head. She missed with all of them. Some of them went out the open window behind Louie's head; some of them hit the wall and broke; others bounced off the wall, miraculously not breaking. These Myra retrieved and winged at him again. Soon Myra was out of bottles.

Louie got out of his chair and climbed onto the roof outside his window. He walked about gathering up the bottles. When he had an armload he climbed back through the window and brought them to Myra, set them at her feet. Then he sat down, lifted his fifth and continued to drink. The bottles began coming at him again. He had another drink, then another drink, then he remembered no more . . .

In the morning Myra awakened first, climbed out of bed, put on coffee, and brought Louie a coffee royal. "Come on," she told him, "I want you to meet my friend Albert. Albert is a very special person."

Louie drank his coffee royal, then they made love. It was good. Louie had a very large knot over his left eye. He got out of bed and dressed. "O.K.," he said, "let's go."

They took the elevator down, walked to Alvarado Street and caught the bus running north. They rode along quietly for five minutes and then Myra reached up and pulled the cord. They got off, walked half a block, then entered an old brown apartment house. They walked up one flight of stairs, around a bend in the

the hall, and Myra stopped at Room 203. She knocked. Footsteps could be heard and the door opened. "Hello, Albert." "Hello, Myra." "Albert, I want you to meet Louie. Louie, this is Albert." They shook hands.

Albert had four hands. He also had four arms to go with them. The top two arms had sleeves and the bottom two arms hung out of holes cut in the shirt.

"Come on in," said Albert. In one of his hands Albert held a drink, a scotch and water. In another hand he held a cigarette. In the third hand he held a newspaper. The fourth hand, the one that had shook Louie's hand, was not occupied with anything. Myra went to the kitchen, got a glass, poured Louie a shot from the bottle in her purse. Then she sat down and began to drink out of the bottle.

"What are you thinking about?" she asked.

"Sometimes you just hit the bottom of terror, you give up, and you still don't die," said Louie.

"Albert raped the fat lady," Myra explained. "You should have seen him with all those arms around her. You were a sight, Albert."

Albert groaned and looked depressed.

"Albert drank himself out of the circus, raped and drank himself right out of the god-damned circus. Now he's on relief."

"Somehow I could never fit into society. I am unfond of humanity. I have no desire to conform, no sense of loyalty, no real purpose."

Albert walked over to the telephone. He held the telephone in one hand, the Daily Racing Form in the second hand, a cigarette in the third and a drink in the fourth.

"Jack? Yeh. This is Albert. Listen, I want Crunchy Main, two win in the first. Give me Blazing Lord, two across in the fourth. Hammerhead Justice, five win in the seventh. And give me Noble Flake, five win and five place in the ninth."

Albert hung up. "My body gnaws at me from one side and my spirit gnaws at me from the other."

"How you doing at the track, Albert?" asked Myra.

"I'm 40 bucks ahead. I got a new play. I figured it out one night when I couldn't sleep. The whole thing opened up to me like a book. If I get any better they won't take my action. Of course I could always go to the track and place my bets there, but . . ."

"But what, Albert?"

"Oh, for Christ's sake . . ."

"What do you mean, Albert?"

"I MEAN PEOPLE STARE! FOR CHRIST'S SAKE DON'T YOU UNDERSTAND?"

"Sorry, Albert."

"Don't be sorry. I don't want your pity!"

"All right. No pity."

"I oughta slap the shit out of you for being so dumb."

"I'll bet you could slap the shit out of me. All those hands."

"Don't tempt me," said Albert.

He finished his drink and walked over and mixed himself another. Then he sat down. Louie hadn't said anything. He felt that he should say something.

"You oughta get into boxing, Albert. Those two extra hands — you'd be a terror."

"Don't be funny, asshole."

Myra poured Louie another drink. They sat around not talking for a while. Then Albert looked up. He looked at Myra. "You fucking this guy?"

"No, I'm not, Albert. I love you, you know that."

"I don't know anything."

"You know I love you, Albert." Myra walked over and sat on Albert's lap. "You're so touchy. I don't pity you, Albert, I love you."

She kissed him.

"I love you, too, baby," said Albert.

"More than any other woman?"

"More than *all* the other women!"

They kissed again. It was a terribly long kiss. That is, it was a terribly long kiss for Louie who sat there with his drink. He reached up and touched the large knot above his left eye. Then his bowels twisted a bit and he went to the bathroom and had a long slow crap.

When he came out Myra and Albert were standing in the center of the room, kissing. Louie sat down and picked up Myra's bottle and watched. While the two top arms held Myra in an embrace the bottom two hands lifted Myra's dress up to her waist and then worked inside her panties. As the panties came down Louie took another drag from the bottle, set it on the floor, got up, walked to the door, and walked out.

★ ★ ★

134

Back at the Red Peacock Louie went to his favorite stool and sat down. The barkeep walked up.

"Well, Louie, how did you make out?"

"Make out?"

"With the lady."

"With the lady?"

"You left together, man. Did you get her?"

"No, not really . . .

"What went wrong?"

"What went wrong?"

"Yes, what went wrong?"

"Give me a whiskey sour, Billy."

Billy walked over and fixed the drink. He brought it back to Louie. Neither of them spoke. Billy walked down to the other end of the bar and stood there. Louie lifted his drink and drank half of it. It was a good drink. He lit a cigarette and held it in one hand. He held the drink in the other hand. The sun was coming in through the door from the street. There was no smog outside. It was going to be a nice day. It was going to be a nicer day than yesterday.

WHITE DOG HUNCH

Henry took the pillow and bunched it behind his back and waited. Louise came in with toast, marmalade and coffee. The toast was buttered.

"Are you sure you don't want a couple of soft-boiled eggs?" she asked.

"No, it's O.K. This is fine."

"You should have a couple of eggs."

"All right, then."

Louise left the bedroom. He'd been up earlier to go to the bathroom and noticed his clothes had been hung up. Something Lita would never do. And Louise was an excellent fuck. No children. He loved the way she did things, softly, carefully. Lita was always on the attack—all hard edges. When Louise came back with the eggs he asked her, "What was it?"

"What was what?"

"You even peeled the eggs. I mean, why did your husband divorce you?"

"Oh, wait," she said, "the coffee is boiling!" and she ran from the room.

He could listen to classical music with her. She played the piano. She had books: *The Savage God* by Alvarez; *The Life of Picasso*; E. B. White; e. e. cummings; T. S. Eliot; Pound; Ibsen, and on and on. She even had nine of his *own* books. Maybe that was the best part.

Louise returned and got into bed, put her plate on her lap. "What went wrong with *your* marriage?"

"Which one? There've been five!"

"The last. Lita."

"Oh. Well, unless Lita was in *motion* she didn't think anything was happening. She liked dancing and parties, her whole life revolved around dancing and parties. She liked what she called 'getting high.' That meant men. She claimed I restricted her 'highs.' She said I was jealous."

"Did you restrict her?"

"I suppose so, but I tried not to. During the last party I went into the backyard with my beer and let her carry on. There was a houseful of men, I could hear her in there squealing, '*Yeehooo! Yee Hoo! Yee Hoo!*' I suppose she was just a natural country girl."

"You could have danced too."

"I suppose so. Sometimes I did. But they turn the stereo up so high that you can't think. I went out into the yard. I went back for some beer and there was a guy kissing her under the stairway. I walked out until they were finished, then went back again for the beer. It was dark but I thought it had been a friend and later I asked him what he was doing under the stairway there."

"Did she love you?"

"She said she did."

"You know, kissing and dancing isn't so bad."

"I suppose not. But you'd have to see her. She had a way of dancing as if she were offering herself as a sacrifice. For rape. It was very effective. The men loved it. She was 33 years old with two children."

"She didn't realize you were a solitary. Men have different natures."

"She never considered my nature. Like I say, unless she was in motion, or turning on, she didn't think anything was happening. Otherwise she was bored. 'Oh, this bores me or that bores me. Eating breakfast with you bores me. Watching you write bores me. I need challenges.'"

"That doesn't seem completely wrong."

"I suppose not. But you know, only boring people get bored. They have to prod themselves continually in order to feel alive."

"Like your drinking, for instance?"

"Yes, like my drinking. I can't face life straight on either."

"Was that all there was to the problem?"

138

"No, she was a nymphomaniac but didn't know it. She claimed I satisfied her sexually but I doubt if I satisfied her spiritual nymphomania. She was the second nymph I had lived with. She had fine qualities aside from that, but her nymphomania was embarrassing. Both to me and to my friends. They'd take me aside and say, 'What the hell's the matter with her?' And I'd say, 'Nothing, she's just a country girl.'"

"Was she?"

"Yes. But the other part was embarrassing."

"More toast?"

"No, this is fine."

"What was embarrassing?"

"Her behavior. If there was another man in the room she'd sit as close to him as possible. He would duck down to put out a cigarette in an ashtray on the floor, she'd duck down too. Then he'd turn his head to look at something and she'd do the same thing."

"Was it a coincidence?"

"I used to think so. But it happened too often. The man would get up to walk across the room and she'd get up and walk right alongside of him. Then when he walked back across the room she'd follow right by his side. The incidents were continuous and numerous, and like I say, embarrassing to both me and my friends. And yet I'm sure she didn't know what she was doing, it all came from the subconscious."

"When I was a girl there was a woman in the neighborhood with this 15-year-old daughter. The daughter was uncontrollable. The mother would send her out for a loaf of bread and she'd come back eight hours later with the bread but meanwhile she would have fucked six men."

"I guess the mother should have baked her own bread."

"I suppose so. The girl couldn't help herself. Whenever she saw a man she'd start to jiggle all over. The mother finally had her spayed."

"Can they do that?"

"Yes, but you have to go through all kinds of legal procedures. There was nothing else to do with her. She'd have been pregnant all her life.

"Do you have anything against dancing?" Louise continued.

"Most people dance for joy, out of good feeling. She crossed

139

over into dirty areas. One of her favorite dances was The White Dog Hunch. A guy would wrap both his legs around her leg and hump her like a male dog in heat. Another of her favorites was The Drunk Dance. She and her partner would end up on the floor rolling over on top of each other."

"She said you were jealous of her dancing?"

"That was the word she used most often: jealous."

"I used to dance in high school."

"Yeah? Listen, thanks for breakfast."

"It's all right. I had a partner in high school. We were the best dancers in school. He had three balls; I thought it was a sign of masculinity."

"Three balls?"

"Yes, three balls. Anyhow, we really knew how to dance. I'd signal by touching him on the wrist, then we'd both leap and turn in the air, very high, and land on our feet. One time we were dancing, I touched his wrist and I made my leap and turn, but I didn't land on my feet. I landed on my ass. He put his hand over his mouth and stared down at me and said, 'Oh, good heavens!' and he walked off. He didn't pick me up. He was a homosexual. We never danced again."

"Do you have something against three-balled homosexuals?"

"No, but we never danced again."

"Lita, she was really dance-obsessed. She'd go into strange bars and ask men to dance with her. Of course, they would. They thought she was an easy fuck. I don't know if she did or didn't. I suppose that sometimes she did. The trouble with men who dance or hang out in bars is that their perception is on a parallel with the tape worm."

"How did you know that?"

"They're caught in the ritual."

"What ritual?"

"The ritual of misdirected energy."

Henry got up and began to dress. "Kid, I got to get going."

"What is it?"

"I just have to get some work done. I'm supposed to be a writer."

"There's a play by Ibsen on tv tonight. 8:30. Will you come over?"

"Sure. I left that pint of scotch. Don't drink it all."

Henry got into his clothes and went down the stairway and got into his car and drove to his place and his typewriter. Second floor rear. Every day as he typed, the woman downstairs would beat on her ceiling with the broom. He wrote the hard way, it had always been the hard way: *The White Dog Hunch* . . .

Louise phoned at 5:30 p.m. She'd been at the scotch. She was drunk. She slurred her words. She rambled. The reader of Thomas Chatterton and D. H. Lawrence. The reader of nine of his books.

"Henry?"

"Yes?"

"Oh, something marvelous has happened!"

"Yes?"

"This black boy came to see me. He's *beautiful!* He's more beautiful than you . . ."

"Of course."

". . . more beautiful than you and I."

"Yes."

"He got me so excited! I'm about to go out of my mind!"

"Yes."

"You don't mind?"

"No."

"You know how we spent the afternoon?"

"No."

"Reading *your poems!*"

"Oh?"

"And you know what he said?"

"No."

"He said your poems were *great!*"

"That's O.K."

"Listen, he got me so *excited.* I don't know how to handle it. Won't you come over? Now? I want to see you now . . ."

"Louise, I'm working . . ."

"Listen, you don't have anything against black men?"

"No."

"I've known this boy for ten years. He used to work for me when I was rich."

"You mean when you were still with your rich husband."

"Will I see you later? Ibsen is on at 8:30."

"I'll let you know."

"Why did that bastard come around? I was all right and then he came around. Christ. I'm so excited, I've got to see you. I'm about to go crazy. He was so *beautiful*."

"I'm working, Louise. The word around here is 'Rent.' Try to understand."

Louise hung up. She called again at 8:20 about Ibsen. Henry said he was still working. He was. Then he began to drink and just sat in a chair, he just sat in a chair. At 9:50 there was a knock on the door. It was Booboo Meltzer, the number one rock star of 1970, currently unemployed, still living off royalties. "Hello, kid," said Henry.

Meltzer walked in and sat down.

"Man," he said, "you're a beautiful old cat. I can't get over you."

"Lay off, kid, cats are out of style, dogs are in now."

"I got a hunch you need help, old man."

"Kid, it's never been different."

Henry walked into the kitchen, found two beers, cracked them and walked out.

"I'm out of cunt, kid, which to me is like being out of love. I can't separate them. I'm not that clever."

"None of us are clever, Pops. We all need help."

"Yeh."

Meltzer had a small celluloid tube. Carefully he tapped out two little white spots on the coffee table.

"This is cocaine, Pops, *cocaine* . . ."

"Ah, hah."

Meltzer reached into his pocket, pulled out a $50 bill, rolled the 50 tightly, then worked it up one nostril. Pressing a finger on the other nostril he bent over one of the white spots on the coffee table and inhaled it. Then he took the $50 bill, worked it up the other nostril and sniffed the second white spot.

"Snow," said Meltzer.

"It's Christmas. Appropriate," said Henry.

Meltzer tapped out two more white spots and passed the fifty. Henry said, "Hold it, I'll use my own," and he found a $1 bill and sniffed up. Once for each nostril

"What do you think of *The White Dog Hunch?*" asked Henry.

"This is 'The White Dog Hunch,'" said Meltzer, tapping out two more spots.

"God," said Henry, "I don't think I'll ever be bored again. You're not bored with me, are you?"

"No way," said Meltzer, sniffing it up through the $50 with all his might. "Pops, there's just no way . . ."

LONG DISTANCE DRUNK

The phone rang at 3 a.m. Francine got up and answered it and brought the phone to Tony in bed. It was Francine's phone. Tony answered. It was Joanna long distance from Frisco. "Listen," he said, "I told you never to phone me here." Joanna had been drinking. "You just shut up and listen to me. You *owe* me something, Tony." Tony exhaled slowly, "O.K., go ahead."

"How's Francine?"

"Nice of you to ask. She's fine. We're both fine. We were asleep."

"Well, anyhow, I got hungry and went for pizza, I went to a pizza parlor."

"Yeh?"

"You've got something against pizza?"

"Pizza is garbage."

"Ah, you don't know what's good. Anyhow, I sat down in the pizza parlor and ordered special pizza. 'Give me the very best,' I told them. I sat there and they brought it and said $18. I said I couldn't pay $18. They laughed and went away and I began to eat the pizza."

"How are your sisters?"

"I don't live with either of them anymore. They both ran me out. It was those long-distance phone calls to you. Some of the phone bills ran over $200."

"I've told you to stop phoning."

"Shut up. It's my way of letting myself down easy. You *owe* me something."

"All right, go ahead."

"Well, anyhow, I got to eating the pizza and wondering how I was going to pay for it. Then I got dry. I needed a beer so I took the pizza to the bar and ordered a beer. I drank that and ate some of the pizza and then I noticed a tall Texan standing next to me. He must have been seven feet tall. He bought me a beer. He was playing music on the juke box and it was country western. It was a country western place. You don't like country western music, do you?"

"It's pizza I dislike."

"Anyhow, I gave the tall Texan some of my pizza and he bought me another beer. We kept drinking beer and eating pizza until the pizza was finished. He paid for the pizza and we went to another bar. Country western again. We danced. He was a good dancer. We drank and kept hitting country western bars. Every bar we went to was country western. We drank beer and danced. He was a great dancer."

"Yes?"

"Finally we got hungry again and we went to a drive-in for a hamburger. We ate our hamburgers and then suddenly he leaned over and kissed me. It was a hot kiss. Wow!"

"Oh?"

"I told him, 'Hell, let's go to a motel.' And he said, 'No, let's go to my place.' And I said, 'No, I want to go to a motel.' But he insisted upon going to his place."

"Was there a wife?"

"No, his wife was in prison. She'd shot and killed one of their daughters, a 17-year-old."

"I see."

"Well, he had one daughter left. She was 16 and he introduced me to his daughter, and then we went into his bedroom."

"Do I have to listen to the details?"

"Let me *talk! I'm* paying for this call! I've paid for *all* these calls! You owe me something, you listen to me!"

"Go ahead."

"Well, we got into the bedroom and stripped down. He was really hung but his pecker looked terribly blue."

"It's when the balls are blue, there's trouble."

"Anyhow, we climbed into bed and played around. But there was a problem . . ."

"Too drunk?"

"Yes. But mainly it was that he only got hot when his daughter

146

came into the room or made a noise—like coughing or flushing the toilet. Any glimpse or sign of his daughter would turn him on, he'd really get hot."

"I understand."

"Do you?"

"Yes."

"Anyhow, in the morning he told me that I had a home for life if I wanted it. Plus a $300-a-week allowance. He has a very nice place: two-and-one-half bathrooms, three or four tv sets, a bookcase full of books: Pearl S. Buck, Agatha Christie, Shakespeare, Proust, Hemingway, the Harvard Classics, hundreds of cookbooks and the Bible. He has two dogs, a cat, three cars . . ."

"Yes?"

"That's all I wanted to tell you. Goodbye."

Joanna hung up. Tony put the receiver back in the cradle, then set the phone on the floor. Tony stretched out. He hoped Francine was asleep. She wasn't. "What'd she want?" she asked.

"She told me a story about a man who fucked his daughters."

"Why? Why should she tell you that?"

"I suppose she thought I'd be interested, plus the fact that she fucked him too."

"Are you?"

"Not really."

Francine turned over to him and he slipped his arm around her. Three a.m. drunks, all over America, were staring at the walls, having finally given it up. You didn't have to be a drunk to get hurt, to be zeroed out by a woman; but you could get hurt and become a drunk. You might think for a while, especially when you were young, that luck was with you, and sometimes it was. But there were all manner of averages and laws working that you knew nothing about, even as you imagined things were going well. Some night, some hot summer Thursday night, *you* became the drunk, *you* were out there alone in a cheap rented room, and no matter how many times you'd been out there before, it was no help, it was even worse because you had got to thinking you wouldn't have to face it again. All you could do was light another cigarette, pour another drink, check the peeling walls for lips and eyes. What men and women did to each other was beyond comprehension.

Tony drew Francine closer to him, pressed his body quietly against hers and listened to her breathe. It was horrible to have to be serious about shit like this once again.

Los Angeles was so strange. He listened. The birds were already up, chirping, yet it was pitch dark. Soon the people would be heading for the freeways. You'd hear the freeways hum, plus cars starting everywhere on the streets. Meanwhile the 3 a.m. drunks of the world would lay in their beds, trying in vain to sleep, and deserving that rest, if they could find it.

HOW TO GET PUBLISHED

Having been an underground writer all of my life I have known some strange editors but the strangest of them all was H. R. Mulloch and his wife, Honeysuckle. Mulloch, ex-con and ex-diamond thief, was editor of the magazine, *Demise*. I began to send him poetry and a correspondence ensued. He claimed my poetry had ruined him for everybody else's poetry; and I wrote back and said it had ruined me for everybody else's poetry, too. H.R. began talking about the possibilities of putting out a book of my poems and I said okay, fine, go ahead. He wrote back, I can't pay royalties, we're as poor as a church mouse. I wrote back, okay, fine, forget royalties, I'm as poor as a church mouse's shriveled titty. He replied, wait a minute, most writers, well, I meet them and they are complete assholes and horrible human beings. I wrote back, you're right, I'm a complete asshole and a horrible human being. O.K., he answered, me and Honeysuckle are coming to L.A. to check you out.

The phone rang a week and a half later. They were in town, just in from New Orleans, staying in a Third Street hotel filled with prostitutes, winos, pickpockets, second story men, dishwashers, muggers, stranglers and rapists. Mulloch loved the low-life, and I think he even loved poverty. From his letters I got the idea that H.R. believed that poverty bred purity. Of course, that's what the rich have always wanted us to believe, but that's another story.

I got in the car with Marie and we drove on down, first stopping for three six-packs and a fifth of cheap whiskey. There was a little grey-haired man about five feet tall standing outside. He was dressed in workingman's blues but with a bandanna (white) about

149

his throat. On his head he wore a very tall white sombrero. Marie and I walked up. He was puffing on a cigarette and smiling. "You Chinaski?" "Yeh." I said, "and this is Marie, my woman." "No man," he answered, "can ever call a woman his own. We never own 'em, we only borrow 'em for a little while." "Yeh," I said, "I guess that's best." We followed H.R. up the stairway down a hall painted blue and red that smelled of murder.

"Only hotel in town we could find that would take the dogs, a parrot, and the two of us."

"Looks like a nice place," I said.

He opened his door and we walked in. There were two dogs in there running around, and Honeysuckle was standing in the center of the room with a parrot on her shoulder.

"Thomas Wolfe," said the parrot, "is the world's greatest living writer."

"Wolfe's dead," I said. "Your parrot is wrong."

"It's an old parrot," said H.R. "We've had him a long time."

"How long have you been with Honeysuckle?"

"Thirty years."

"Just borrowed her for a while?"

"That's the way it seems."

The dogs ran around and Honeysuckle stood in the center of the room with the parrot on her shoulder. She looked dark, Italian or Greek, very skinny, with pouches under her eyes; she looked tragic and kind and dangerous, mostly tragic. I put the whiskey and beer on the table and everybody moved forward toward it. H.R. began ripping off beercaps and I started peeling the whiskey. Dusty drinking glasses appeared along with several ashtrays. Through the wall to the left, a male voice suddenly boomed, "You fuckin' whore I want you to eat my shit!"

We sat down and I splashed the whiskey around. H.R. passed me a cigar. I peeled it, bit off the end and lit up.

"What'cha think of modern literature?" H.R. asked me.

"Don't really care for it."

H.R. narrowed his eyes and grinned at me. "Ha, I thought so!"

"Listen," I said, "why don't you take off that sombrero so I can see who I'm dealing with. You might be a horse thief."

"No," he said, sweeping the sombrero off with a dramatic gesture, "but I was one of the best diamond thieves in the state of Ohio."

"Is that so?"

"It is."

The girls were drinking away. "I just love my dogs," said Honeysuckle. "Do you love dogs?" she asked me.

"I don't know if I love them or not."

"He loves himself," said Marie.

"Marie has a very penetrating mind," I said.

"I like the way you write," said H.R. "You can say a lot without getting fancy."

"Genius might be the ability to say a profound thing in a simple way."

"What's that?" H.R. asked.

I repeated the statement and splashed more whiskey around.

"I gotta write that down," said H.R. He pulled a pen from his pocket and wrote it down on the edge of one of the brown paper bags laying on the table.

The parrot climbed off Honeysuckle's shoulder, walked across the table and climbed up on my left shoulder. "That's nice," said Honeysuckle. "James Thurber," said the bird, "is the world's greatest living writer." "Dumb bastard," I said to the bird. I felt a sharp pain in my left ear. The bird had almost torn it off. We are all such sensitive creatures. H.R. ripped off more beercaps. We drank on.

Afternoon became evening and evening became night. I awakened in the dark. I had been sleeping on the rug in the center of the floor. H.R. and Honeysuckle were asleep in the bed. Marie was asleep on the couch. All three of them snored, especially Marie. I got up and sat at the table. There was some whiskey left. I poured it and drank a warm beer. I sat there and drank some more warm beer. The parrot sat on the back of a chair across from me. Suddenly he climbed down and walked across the table between the ashtrays and empty bottles and climbed up on my shoulder. "Don't say that thing," I told him, "it's very irritating to me when you say that thing." "Fuckin' whore," said the parrot. I lifted the bird by its feet and placed him back on the chair. Then I got back down on the rug and went to sleep.

In the morning, H.R. Mulloch made an announcement. "I've decided to print a book of your poems. We might as well go home and get to work."

"You mean you realized I'm not a horrible human being?"

"No," said H.R., "I didn't realize that at all, but I've decided to ignore my better judgment and print you anyhow."

"Were you really the best diamond thief in the state of Ohio?"

"Oh, yes."

"I know you did time. How'd you get caught?"

"It was so stupid I don't want to talk about it."

I went down and got a couple more six packs and came back and Marie and I helped H.R. and Honeysuckle pack. There were special carrying cases for the dogs and the parrot. We got everything down the stairway and into my car, then we sat and finished the beer. We were all pros: nobody was foolish enough to suggest breakfast.

"You come out and see us now," said H.R. "We're going to be putting the book together. You're a son of a bitch but a man can talk to you. Those other poets, they're always flaunting their feathers and putting on a dumb asshole act."

"You're okay," said Honeysuckle. "The dogs like you."

"And the parrot," said H.R.

The girls stayed in the car and I went back with H.R. while he turned in his key. An old woman in a green kimono, her hair dyed a bright red, opened the door.

"This is Mama Stafford," H.R. said to me. "Mama Stafford, this is the world's greatest poet."

"Really?" asked Mama.

"The world's greatest living poet," I said.

"Why don't you boys come in for a drink? You look like you need one."

We went in and each of us forced down a glass of warm white wine. We said goodbye and went back to the car . . .

At the train station, H.R. got the tickets and checked in the parrot and dogs at the baggage counter. Then he came back and sat down with us. "Hate flying," he said. "Terrified of flying." I went and got a half pint and we passed it around waiting. Then they started loading the train. We stood around on the platform and suddenly Honeysuckle leaped on me and gave me a long kiss. Toward the end of the kiss she passed her tongue rapidly in and out of my mouth. I stood and lit a cigar while Marie kissed H.R. Then H.R. and Honeysuckle climbed into the train.

152

"He's a nice man," said Marie.

"Sweetie," I said, "I think you gave him rocks."

"Are you jealous?"

"I'm always jealous."

"Look, they're sitting at the window, they're smiling at us."

"It's embarrassing. I wish the fucking train would pull out."

Finally the train did begin to pull out. We waved, of course, and they waved back. H.R. had a pleased and happy grin. Honeysuckle seemed to be crying. She looked quite tragic. Then we couldn't see them anymore. It was over. I was about to be published. Selected Poems. We turned and walked back through the train station.

SPIDER

When I rang he was on his sixth or seventh beer and I walked to
the refrigerator and got one for myself. Then I came out and sat
down. He looked really low.

"What is it, Max?"

"I just lost one. She left a couple of hours ago."

"I don't know what to say, Max."

He looked up from his beer. "Listen, I know you're not going to
believe this, but I haven't had a piece of ass in four years."

I sucked at my beer. "I believe you, Max. In fact, in our society
there are a great number of people who go from cradle to grave
without any ass at all. They sit in tiny rooms and make objects
out of tinfoil which they hang in the window and watch while the
sun glints on them, watch them twist in the wind . . ."

"Well, I just lost one. And she was right here . . ."

"Tell me about it."

"Well, the doorbell rang and there stood a young girl, blonde, in
a white dress with blue shoes, and she said, 'Are you Max
Miklovik?' I told her I was and she said she had read my shit and
would I let her in? I told her I would, really, and I let her in and
she walked over to a chair in the corner and sat down. I walked
into the kitchen and poured two whiskey and waters, walked back
out, gave her one and then walked over and sat on the couch."

"A looker?" I asked.

"A real looker and a good body, that dress didn't hide a thing.
Then she asked me, 'You ever read Jerzy Kosinski?' 'I read his
Painted Bird,' I said. 'A terrible writer.' 'He's a very good writer,'
she said."

Max just sat there, thinking about Kosinski, I guess. "Then what happened?" I asked.

"There was a spider weaving a web up above her. She gave a little scream. She said, 'That spider shit on me!'"

"Did it?"

"I told her that spiders didn't shit. She said, 'Yes, they do.' And I said, 'Jerzy Kosinski's a spider,' and she said, 'My name's Lyn,' and I said, 'Hello, Lyn.'"

"Some conversation."

"Some conversation. Then she said, 'I want to tell you something.' And I said, 'Go ahead.' And she said, 'I was taught to play the piano at the age of 13 by a real count, I saw his papers, he was legitimate, a real count. Count Rudolph Stauffer.' 'Drink up, drink up,' I told her."

"Can I have another beer, Max?"

"Sure, bring me one."

When I came back he continued. "She finished her drink and I went over to get her glass. As I reached for her glass I leaned over to kiss her. She pulled away. 'Shit, what's a kiss?' I asked her. 'Spiders kiss.'"

"'Spiders don't kiss,' she said. There was nothing to do but go in and mix two more drinks, a bit stronger. I came out, handed Lyn a drink and sat down on the couch again."

"I suppose you both should have been on the couch," I said.

"But we weren't. And she went on talking. 'The Count,' she said, 'had a high forehead, hazel eyes, pink hair, long thin fingers and he always smelled of semen.'"

"Ah."

"She said, 'He was 65 but he was hot. He taught my mother the piano too. My mother was 35 and I was 13 and he taught us both the piano.'"

"What were you supposed to say to that?" I asked.

"I don't know. So I told her, 'Kosinski can't write shit.' And she said, 'He made love to my mother.' And I said, 'Who? Kosinski?' And she said, 'No, the Count.' 'Did the Count fuck you?' I asked her. And she said, 'No, he never fucked me. But he touched me in various places, he made me very excited. And he played *marvelous* piano.'"

156

"How did you respond to all that?"

"Well, I told her about the time I worked for the Red Cross during the Second World War. We went around and collected bottles of blood. There was a nurse there, black hair, very fat, and after lunch she'd lay on the lawn with her legs opened toward me. She'd stare and stare. After we collected the blood I'd take the bottles to the storage room. It was cold in there and the bottles were kept in little white sacks and sometimes when I handed them to the girl in charge of the storage room a bottle would slip out of its sack and break on the floor. SPOW! Blood and glass everywhere. But the girl always said, 'That's all right, don't worry about it.' I thought she was very kind and I took to kissing her when I delivered the blood. It was very nice kissing her inside that refrigerator but I never got anywhere with the one with black hair who laid on the grass after lunch and opened her legs at me."

"You told her that?"

"I told her that."

"And what did she say?"

"She said, 'That spider's coming down! It's coming down on me!' 'O, my god,' I said and I grabbed the *Racing Form* and opened it and caught the spider between the third race for maiden three-year-olds at six furlongs and the fourth race which was a five thousand dollar claimer for four-year-olds-and-up at a mile-and-one-sixteenth. I threw the paper down and managed to give Lyn a quick kiss. She didn't respond."

"What did she say about the kiss?"

"She said that her father was a genius in the computer industry and he was seldom home but somehow he found out about her mother and the Count. He got hold of her one day after school and took her head and beat it against the wall, asking her why she had covered up for her mother. It made her father very angry when he found out the truth. He finally stopped beating her head against the wall and went in and beat her mother's head against the wall. She said it was horrible and they never saw the Count again."

"What did you say to that?"

"I told her that once I met this woman in a bar and I took her home. When she took off her panties there was so much blood and shit in them that I couldn't do it. She smelled like an oil well.

157

She gave me a back rub with olive oil and I gave her five dollars, a half bottle of stale port wine, the address of my best friend and I sent her on her way."

"Did that really happen?"

"Yeah. Then this Lyn asked me if I liked T. S. Eliot. I told her I didn't. Then she said, 'I like your writing, Max, it's so ugly and demented that it fascinates me. I was in love with you. I wrote you letter after letter but you never answered.' 'Sorry, baby,' I said. She said, 'I went crazy. I went to Mexico. I got religion. I wore a black shawl and went singing in the streets at 3 a.m. Nobody bothered me. I had all your books in my suitcase and I drank tequila and lit candles. Then I met this matador and he made me forget you. It lasted several weeks.' "

"Those guys get plenty of pussy."

"I know," Max said. "Anyhow, she said they finally got tired of each other and I said, 'Let me be your matador.' And she said, 'You're like every other man. All you want to do is fuck.' 'Suck and fuck,' I told her. I walked over to her. 'Kiss me,' I said. 'Max,' she said, 'all you want to do is to play. You don't care for *me*.' 'I care for me,' I answered. 'If you weren't such a great writer,' she said, 'no woman would even talk to you.' 'Let's fuck,' I said. 'I want you to marry me,' she said. 'I don't want to marry you,' I said. She picked up her purse and walked out."

"That's the end of the story?" I asked.

"That's it," said Max, "no ass in four years and I lose that one. Pride, stupidity, whatever."

"You're a good writer, Max, but you're no ladies' man."

"You think a good ladies' man could have worked it?"

"Sure, you see each of her gambits must be parried with the correct response. Each correct response turns the conversation in a new direction until the ladies' man has the woman backed into a corner or, more properly, flat upon her back."

"How can I learn?"

"There's no learning. It's an instinct. You have to know what a woman is really saying when she is saying something else. It can't be taught."

"What did she really say?"

"She wanted you but you didn't know how to get to her. You couldn't build a bridge. You flopped, Max."

"But she'd read all my books. She thought I knew something."

"*Now* she knows something."

"What?"

"That you're a dumb ass, Max."

"Am I?"

"All writers are dumb asses. That's why they write things down."

"What do you mean, 'That's why they write things down'?"

"I mean, they write things down because they don't understand them."

"I write a lot of things down," said Max sadly.

"I remember when I was a kid I read this book by Hemingway. A guy climbed into bed with this woman again and again and he couldn't do it although he loved the woman and she loved him. My god, I thought, what a great book. All these centuries and nobody has written about this aspect of the thing. I thought the guy was just too blissfully dumb-ass to do it. Later on I read in the book that he'd had his genitals shot off in the war. What a let-down."

"You think that girl will be back?" Max asked me. "You should have seen that body, that face, those eyes."

"She won't be back," I said, standing up.

"But what'll I do?" asked Max.

"Just go on writing your pitiful poems and stories and novels . . ."

I left him there and walked down the stairway. There was no more I could say to him. It was 7:45 p.m. and I hadn't had dinner. I got into my car and drove over toward McDonald's, thinking that I'd probably go for the fried shrimp.

THE DEATH OF THE FATHER I

My father's funeral was a cold hamburger. I sat across from the funeral parlor in Alhambra and had a coffee. It would be a short drive to the race track after it was over. A man with a terrible peeling face, very round glasses with thick lenses, walked in. "Henry," he said to me, then sat down and ordered a coffee.

"Hello, Bert."

"Your father and I became very good friends. We talked about you a lot."

"I didn't like my old man," I said.

"Your father loved you, Henry. He was hoping you'd marry Rita." Rita was Bert's daughter. "She's going with the *nicest* guy now but he doesn't excite her. She seems to go for phonies. I don't understand. But she must like him a little," he said, brightening up, "because she hides her baby in the closet when he comes by."

"Come on, Bert, let's go."

We walked across the street and into the funeral parlor. Somebody was saying what a good man my father had been. I felt like telling them the other part. Then somebody sang. We stood and filed past the coffin. I was last. Maybe I'll spit on him, I thought.

My mother was dead. I had buried her the year before, gone to the race track and got laid afterwards. The line moved. Then a woman screamed. "No, no, no! He can't be dead!" She reached down into the casket, lifted his head and kissed him. Nobody stopped her. Her lips were on his. I took my father by the neck and the woman by the neck and pulled them apart. My father fell back into the casket and the woman was led out, trembling.

"That was your father's girlfriend," said Bert.

"Not a bad looker," I said.

When I walked down the steps after the service the woman was waiting. She ran up to me.

"You look just *like* him! You *are* him!"

"No," I said, "he's dead, and I'm younger and nicer."

She put her arms around me and kissed me. I pushed my tongue between her lips. Then I pulled away. "Here, here," I said in a loud voice, "get ahold of yourself!" She kissed me again and this time I worked my tongue deeper into her mouth. My penis was beginning to get hard. Some men and a woman came up to take her away.

"No," she said, "I want to go with him. I must talk to his son!"

"Now, Maria, please, come with us!"

"No, no, I must talk to his son!"

"Do you mind?" a man asked me.

"It's all right," I said.

Maria got into my car and we drove to my father's house. I opened the door and we walked in. "Look around," I said. "You can have any of his stuff you want. I'm going to take a bath. Funerals make me sweat."

When I came out Maria was sitting on the edge of my father's bed.

"Oh, you're wearing his robe!"

"It's mine now."

"He just *loved* that robe. I gave it to him for Christmas. He was so proud of it. He said he was going to wear it and walk around the block for all the neighbors to see."

"Did he?"

"No."

"It is a nice robe. It's mine now."

I took a pack of cigarettes from the night stand.

"Oh, those are his cigarettes!"

"Want one?"

"No."

I lit up. "How long did you know him?"

"About a year."

"And you didn't find out?"

"Find out what?"

"That he was an ignorant man. Cruel. Patriotic. Money hungry. A liar. A coward. A cheat."

162

"No."

"I'm surprised. You look like an intelligent woman."

"I loved your father, Henry."

"How old are you?"

"Forty-three."

"You're well preserved. You have lovely legs."

"Thank you."

"Sexy legs."

I went into the kitchen and got a bottle of wine out of the cupboard, pulled the cork, found two wine glasses and walked back in. I poured her a drink and handed her the glass.

"Your father spoke of you often."

"Yes?"

"He said you lacked ambition."

"He was right."

"Really?"

"My only ambition is not to be anything at all; it seems the most sensible thing."

"You're strange."

"No, my father was strange. Let me pour you another drink. This is good wine."

"He said you were a drunkard."

"You see, I *have* achieved something."

"You look so much like him."

"That's just on the surface. He liked soft-boiled eggs, I like hard. He liked company, I like solitude. He liked to sleep nights, I like to sleep days. He liked dogs, I used to yank their ears and stick matches up their ass. He liked his job, I like to lay around."

I reached over and grabbed Maria. I worked her lips open, got my mouth inside of hers and began to suck the air out of her lungs. I spit down her throat and ran my finger up the crack of her ass. We broke apart.

"He kissed me gently," said Maria. "He loved me."

"Shit," I said, "my mother was underground only a month before he was sucking your nipples and sharing your toilet paper."

"He loved me."

"Balls. His fear of being alone led him to your vagina."

"He said you were a bitter young man."

"Hell, yes. Look what I had for a father."

I pulled up her dress and began kissing her legs. I began at the knees. I got to the inner thigh and she opened up for me. I bit her, hard, and she jumped and farted. "Oh, I'm sorry." "It's all right," I said.

I fixed her another drink, lit one of my dead father's cigarettes and went into the kitchen for a second bottle of wine. We drank another hour or two. The afternoon was just turning into evening but I was weary. Death was so dull. That was the worst thing about death. It was dull. Once it happened there wasn't anything you could do. You couldn't play tennis with it or turn it into a box of bonbons. It was there like a flat tire was there. Death was stupid. I climbed into bed. I heard Maria taking off her shoes, her clothes, then I felt her in bed beside me. Her head was on my chest and I felt my fingers rubbing her behind the ears. Then my penis began to rise. I lifted her head and put my mouth on hers. I put it there gently. Then I took her hand and placed it on my cock.

I had drunk too much wine. I mounted her. I stroked and stroked. I was always on the verge but I couldn't arrive. I was giving her a long sweaty neverending horsefuck. The bed jerked and bounced, jiggled and moaned. Maria moaned. I kissed her and kissed her. Her mouth gasped for air. "My god," she said, "you're REALLY FUCKING me!" I only wanted to finish but the wine had dulled the mechanism. Finally I rolled off.

"God," she said. "God."

We began kissing and it started all over again. I mounted once more. This time I felt the climax slowly arriving. "Oh," I said, "oh, Christ!" I finally made it, got up, went to the bathroom, came out, smoking a cigarette and went back to the bed. She was almost asleep. "My god," she said, "you really FUCKED me!" We slept.

In the morning I got up, vomited, brushed my teeth, gargled, and cracked a bottle of beer. Maria awakened and looked at me.

"Did we fuck?" she asked.

"Are you serious?"

"No, I want to know. Did we fuck?"

"No," I said, "nothing happened."

Maria went into the bathroom and showered. She sang. Then she toweled and came out. She looked at me. "I feel like a woman who's been fucked."

"Nothing happened, Maria."

We got dressed and I took her to a cafe around the corner. She had sausage and scrambled eggs, wheat toast, coffee. I had a glass of tomato juice and a bran muffin.

"I can't get over it. You look just like him."

"Not this morning, Maria, please."

While I was watching Maria put scrambled eggs and sausage and wheat toast (spread with raspberry jam) into her mouth I realized that we had missed the burial. We had forgotten to drive to the cemetery to watch the old man dropped into the hole. I had wanted to see that. That was the only good part of the thing. We hadn't joined the funeral procession, instead we had gone to my father's house and smoked his cigarettes and drunk his wine.

Maria put a particularly large mouthful of bright yellow scrambled egg into her mouth and said, "You must have fucked me. I can feel your semen running down my leg."

"Oh, that's just sweat. It's very hot this morning."

I saw her reach down under the table and under her dress. A finger came back up. She sniffed it. "That's not sweat, that's semen."

Maria finished eating and we left. She gave me her address and I drove her there. I parked at the curbing. "Care to come in?"

"Not just now. I've got to take care of things. The Estate."

Maria leaned over and kissed me. Her eyes were large, stricken, stale. "I know you're much younger but I could love you," she said. "I'm sure I could."

When she got to her doorway she turned. We both waved. I drove to the nearest liquor store, got a half pint and the day's *Racing Form*. I looked forward to a good day at the track. I always did better after a day off.

THE DEATH OF THE FATHER II

My mother had died a year earlier. A week after my father's death I stood in his house alone. It was in Arcadia, and the nearest I had come to the house in some time was passing by on the freeway on my way to Santa Anita.

I was unknown to the neighbors. The funeral was over, and I walked to the sink, poured a glass of water, drank it, then went outside. Not knowing what else to do, I picked up the hose, turned on the water and began watering the shrubbery. Curtains drew back as I stood on the front lawn. Then they began coming out of their houses. A woman walked over from across the street.

"Are you Henry?" she asked me.

I told her that I was Henry.

"We knew your father for years."

Then her husband walked over. "We knew your mother too," he said.

I bent over and shut off the hose. "Won't you come in?" I asked. They introduced themselves as Tom and Nellie Miller and we went into the house.

"You look just like your father."

"Yes, so they tell me."

We sat and looked at each other.

"Oh," said the woman, "he had so *many* pictures. He must have liked pictures."

"Yes, he did, didn't he?"

"I just love that painting of the windmill in the sunset."

"You can have it."

"Oh, can I?"

The doorbell rang. It was the Gibsons. The Gibsons told me that they also had been neighbors of my father's for years.

"You look just like your father," said Mrs. Gibson.

"Henry has given us the painting of the windmill."

"That's nice. I *love* that painting of the blue horse."

"You can have it, Mrs. Gibson."

"Oh, you don't mean it?"

"Yes, it's all right."

The doorbell rang again and another couple came in. I left the door ajar. Soon a single man stuck his head inside. "I'm Doug Hudson. My wife's at the hairdresser's."

"Come in, Mr. Hudson."

Others arrived, mostly in pairs. They began to circulate through the house.

"Are you going to sell the place?"

"I think I will."

"It's a lovely neighborhood."

"I can see that."

"Oh, I just *love* this frame but I don't like the picture."

"Take the frame."

"But what should I do with the picture?"

"Throw it in the trash." I looked around. "If anybody sees a picture they like, please take it."

They did. Soon the walls were bare.

"Do you need these chairs?"

"No, not really."

Passersby were coming in from the street, and not even bothering to introduce themselves.

"How about the sofa?" someone asked in a very loud voice. "Do you want it?"

"I don't want the sofa," I said.

They took the sofa, then the breakfast nook table and chairs.

"You have a toaster here somewhere, don't you, Henry?"

They took the toaster.

"You don't need these dishes, do you?"

"No."

"And the silverware?"

"No."

168

"How about the coffee pot and the blender?"

"Take them."

One of the ladies opened a cupboard on the back porch. "What about all these preserved fruits? You'll never be able to eat all these."

"All right, everybody, take some. But try to divide them equally."

"Oh, I want the strawberries!"

"Oh, I want the figs!"

"Oh, I want the marmalade!"

People kept leaving and returning, bringing new people with them.

"Hey, here's a fifth of whiskey in the cupboard! Do you drink, Henry?"

"Leave the whiskey."

The house was getting crowded. The toilet flushed. Somebody knocked a glass from the sink and broke it.

"You better save this vacuum cleaner, Henry. You can use it for your apartment."

"All right, I'll keep it."

"He had some garden tools in the garage. How about the garden tools?"

"No, I better keep those."

"I'll give you $15 for the garden tools."

"O.K."

He gave me the $15 and I gave him the key to the garage. Soon you could hear him rolling the lawn mower across the street to his place.

"You shouldn't have given him all that equipment for $15, Henry. It was worth much more than that."

I didn't answer.

"How about the car? It's four years old."

"I think I'll keep the car."

"I'll give you $50 for it."

"I think I'll keep the car."

Somebody rolled up the rug in the front room. After that people began to lose interest. Soon there were only three or four left, then they were all gone. They left me the garden hose, the bed, the refrigerator and stove, and a roll of toilet paper.

I walked outside and locked the garage door. Two small boys came by on roller skates. They stopped as I was locking the garage doors.

"See that man?"

"Yes."

"His father died."

They skated on. I picked up the hose, turned the faucet on and began to water the roses.

HARRY ANN LANDERS

The phone rang. It was the writer, Paul. Paul was depressed. Paul was in Northridge.

"Harry?"

"Yeh?"

"Nancy and I broke up."

"Yeh?"

"Listen, I want to get back with her. Can you help me? Unless *you* want to get back with her?"

Harry smiled into the telephone. "I don't want to get back with her, Paul."

"I don't know what went wrong. She started on the money thing. She started hollering about money. She waved phone bills in my face. Listen, I been hustling. I got this act. Barney and I, we're both dressed in penguin suits . . . he says one line of a poem, I say the other . . . four microphones . . . we got this jazz group playing in back of us . . ."

"Phone bills, Paul, can be distracting," said Harry. "You ought to stay off her line when you're juiced. You know too many people in Maine, Boston and New Hampshire. Nancy is an anxiety-neurosis case. She can't start her car without having a fit. She straps herself in, starts trembling and honking her horn. Mad as a hatter. And it extends into other areas. She can't go into a Thrifty Drugstore without getting offended by a stockboy chewing on a Mars candy bar."

"She says she supported *you* for three months."

"She supported my cock. Mostly with credit cards."

"Are you as good as they say you are?"

Harry laughed. "I give them soul. That can't be measured in inches."

"I want to get back with her. Tell me what to do?"

"Either suck pussy like a man or find a job."

"But *you* don't work."

"Don't measure yourself by me. That's the mistake most people make."

"But where can I get some coin? I've really hustled. What am I going to do?"

"Suck air."

"Don't you know anything about mercy?"

"The only people who know about mercy are the ones who need it."

"You'll need mercy some day."

"I need it now—it's just that I need it in a form different than you do."

"I need coin, Harry, how am I going to make it?"

"Shoot the 30-foot basket. A three-pointer. If you make it you're in the clear. If you miss, you got yourself a jail cell—no light bills, no phone bills, no gas bills, no bitching females. You can learn a trade and you earn four cents an hour."

"You can really lay the shit on a man."

"O.K., get the candy out of your ass and I'll tell you something."

"It's out."

"I'd say the reason Nancy dropped you is another guy. Black, white, red or yellow. Note this rule and you'll always be covered: a female seldom moves away from one victim without having another near at hand."

"Man," said Paul, "I need help, not theory."

"Unless you understand the theory you'll always need help . . ."

Harry picked up the phone, dialed Nancy's number.

"Hello?" she answered.

"It's Harry."

"Oh."

"I hear through the vine you got taken in Mexico. Did he get it all?"

"Oh, that . . ."

"A washed-up Spanish bullfighter, wasn't it?"

"With the most *beautiful* eyes. Not like yours. Nobody can *see* your eyes."

"I don't want anybody to see my eyes."

"Why not?"

"If they saw what I was thinking, I couldn't fool them."

"So, you've phoned to tell me you're running with blinkers on?"

"You know that. What I called for is to tell you that Paul wants to come back. Does that help you in any way?"

"No."

"I thought so."

"Did he really phone you?"

"Yes."

"Oh, I've got a new man now. He's marvelous!"

"I told Paul you were probably interested in somebody else."

"How did you know?"

"I knew."

"Harry?"

"Yeh, doll?"

"Go fuck yourself . . ."

Nancy hung up.

Now there, he thought, I *try* to be the peacemaker and both of them get pissed. Harry walked into the bathroom and looked at his face in the mirror. My god, he had a kind face. Couldn't they see that? Understanding. Nobility. He spotted a blackhead in near his nose. He squeezed. Out it came, black and lovely, dragging a yellow tail of pus. The breakthrough, he thought, is in understanding women and love. He rolled the blackhead and the pus between his fingers. Or maybe the breakthrough was the ability to kill without caring. He sat down to take a shit while he thought it over.

BEER AT THE CORNER BAR

I don't know how many years ago it was, 15 or 20. I was sitting in my place. It was a hot summer night and I felt dull.

I walked out the door and down the street. It was past dinner time for most families and they sat about watching their tv sets. I walked up to the boulevard. Across the street was a neighborhood bar, an old-fashioned building and bar constructed of wood, painted green and white. I walked in.

After nearly a lifetime spent in bars I had entirely lost my feeling for them. When I wanted something to drink I usually got it at a liquor store, took it home and drank alone.

I walked in and found a stool away from the crowd. I wasn't ill at ease, I simply felt out of place. But if I wanted to go out there was nowhere else for me to go. In our society most of the interesting places to go are either against the law or very expensive.

I ordered a bottle of beer and lit a cigarette. It was just another neighborhood bar. They all knew each other. They told dirty jokes and watched tv. There was only one woman in there, old, in a black dress, red wig. She had on a dozen necklaces and kept lighting her cigarette over and over again. I began to wish I was back in my room and decided to go there after I finished my beer.

A man came in and took the barstool next to mine. I didn't look up, I wasn't interested, but from his voice I imagined him to be about my age. They knew him in the bar. The bartender called him by name and a couple of the regulars said hello. He sat next to me with his beer for three or four minutes; then he said, "Hi, how ya doin'?"

"I'm doing O.K."

"You new in the neighborhood?"

"No."

"I haven't seen you in here before."

I didn't answer.

"You from Los Angeles?" he asked.

"Mostly."

"You think the Dodgers will make it this year?"

"No."

"You don't like the Dodgers?"

"No."

"Who do you like?"

"Nobody. I don't like baseball."

"What do you like?"

"Boxing. Bullfighting."

"Bullfighting's cruel."

"Yes, anything is cruel when you lose."

"But the bull doesn't stand a chance."

"None of us do."

"You're pretty goddamned negative. Do you believe in God?"

"Not your kind of god."

"What kind?"

"I'm not sure."

"I've been going to church ever since I can remember."

I didn't answer.

"Can I buy you a beer?" he asked.

"Sure."

The beers arrived.

"Did you read the papers today?" he asked.

"Yes."

"Did you read about those 50 little girls who were burned to death in that Boston orphanage?"

"Yes."

"Wasn't that horrible?"

"I suppose it was."

"You *suppose* it was?"

"Yes."

"Don't you *know?*"

"If I had been there I suppose I would have had nightmares about it for the rest of my life. But it's different when you just read about it in the newspapers."

"Don't you feel sorrow for those 50 little girls who burned to death? They were hanging out of the windows screaming."

"I suppose it was horrible. But you see it was just a newspaper headline, a newspaper story. I really didn't think much about it. I turned the page."

"You mean you didn't feel anything?"

"Not really."

He sat a moment and had a drink of his beer. Then he screamed, *"Hey, here's a guy who says he didn't feel a fucking thing when he read about those 50 little orphan girls burning to death in Boston!"*

Everyone looked at me. I looked down at my cigarette. There was a minute of silence. Then the woman in the red wig said, "If I was a man I'd kick his ass all up and down the street."

"He don't believe in God either!" said the guy next to me. *"He hates baseball. He loves bullfights, and he likes to see little orphan girls burned to death!"*

I ordered another beer from the bartender, for myself. He pushed the bottle at me with repugnance. Two young guys were playing pool. The youngest, a big kid in a white t-shirt, laid his stick down and walked over to me. He stood behind me sucking air into his lungs, trying to make his chest bigger.

"This is a nice bar. We don't tolerate assholes in here. We kick their butts good, we beat the shit out of them, we beat the living shit out of them!"

I could feel him standing there behind me. I lifted my beer bottle and poured beer into my glass, drank it, lit a cigarette. My hand was perfectly steady. He stood there for some time, then finally walked back to the pool table. The man who had been sitting next to me got off his stool and moved away. "The son of a bitch is negative," I heard him say. "He hates people."

"If I was a man," said the woman in the red wig, "I'd make him beg for mercy. I can't stand bastards like him."

"That's how guys like Hitler talk," said somebody.

"Real hateful jerks."

I drank that beer, ordered another. The two young guys continued to shoot pool. Some people left and the remarks about me began to die down except in the case of the woman in the red wig. She got drunker.

"Prick, prick . . . you're a real prick! You stink like a cesspool! Betcha hate your country, too, don't you? Your country and your mother and everybody else. Aw, I know you guys! Pricks, cheap cowardly pricks!"

She finally left about 1:30 a.m. One of the kids shooting pool left. The kid in the white t-shirt sat down at the end of the bar and talked to the guy who had bought me the beer. At five minutes to two, I got up slowly and walked out.

Nobody followed me. I walked up the boulevard, found my street. The lights in the houses and the apartments were out. I found my front court. I opened my door and walked in. There was one beer in the refrigerator. I opened it and drank it.

Then I undressed, went to the bathroom, pissed, brushed my teeth, turned out the light, walked to the bed, went to bed and slept.

THE UPWARD BIRD

We were going to interview the well-known poetess, Janice Altrice.
The editor of *America in Poetry* was paying me $175 to write her
up. Tony accompanied me with his camera. He was to get $50 for
the photographs. I had borrowed a tape recorder. The place was
back in the hills up a long road. I pulled the car over, took a pull
of vodka and passed the bottle to Tony.

"Does she drink?" asked Tony.

"Probably not," I said.

I started the car and we went on. We turned right up a narrow
dirt road. Janice was standing in front waiting for us. She was
dressed in slacks and wore a white blouse with a high lace collar.
We climbed out of the car and walked toward where she stood on
the slope of lawn. We introduced ourselves and I started the battery-
operated tape recorder.

"Tony's going to take some shots of you," I told her, "be natural."

"Of course," she said.

We walked up the slope and she pointed to the house. "We bought
it when prices were very low. We couldn't afford it now." Then she
pointed to a smaller house on the side of the hill. "That's my study,
we built it ourselves. It even has a bathroom. Come and see it."

We followed her. She pointed again. "Those flowerbeds. We put
them in ourselves. We're really good with flowers."

"Beautiful," said Tony.

She opened the door to her study and we went in. It was large
and cool with fine Indian blankets and artifacts on the walls. There
was a fireplace, the bookcase, a large desk with an electric

179

typewriter, an unabridged dictionary, typing paper, notebooks. She was small with a very short haircut. Her eyebrows were thick. She smiled often. At the corner of one eye was a deep scar that looked as if it had been etched with a penknife.

"Let's see," I said, "you're five-feet-one and you weigh . . .?"

"One hundred fifteen."

"Age?"

Janice laughed as Tony took her photo. "It's a woman's prerogative not to answer that question." She laughed again. "Just say that I'm ageless."

She was a grand-looking woman. I could see her behind the podium at some college, reading her poems, answering questions, preparing a new generation of poets, pointing them toward life. She probably had good legs, too. I tried to imagine her in bed but I couldn't.

"What are you thinking about?" she asked me.

"Are you intuitive?"

"Of course. I'll put on some coffee. You both need something to drink."

"You're right."

Janice prepared the coffee and we stepped outside. We went out a side door. There was a miniature playground, swings and trapezes, sandpiles, things of that sort. A young lad of about ten came running down the slope. "That's Jason, my youngest, my baby," said Janice from the doorway.

Jason was a tousled-haired young god, blonde, in short pants and a loose purple blouse. His shoes were gold and blue. He appeared to be healthy and lively.

"Mama, Mama! Push me in the swing! Push, push!" Jason ran to the swing, got in and waited.

"Not now, Jason, we're busy."

"Pushy, pushy, Mama!"

"Not now, Jason . . ."

"MAMA MAMA MAMA MAMA MAMA MAMA MAMA," screamed Jason.

Janice walked over and began to push Jason. Back and forth he went, up and down. We waited. After quite a while they finished and Jason slid off. A thick green stream of snot ran from one nostril. He walked up to me. "I like to play with myself," he said, then he ran off.

180

"We don't inhibit him," said Janice. She stared out over the hills, dreamily. "We used to ride horses here. We fought the land developers. Now the outside world is creeping closer and closer. It's still lovely, though. It was after I fell off a horse and broke my leg that I wrote my book, *The Upward Bird, A Chorus of Magic*."

"Yes, I remember," said Tony.

"I planted that redwood 25 years ago," she pointed. "We were the only house here in those days, but things change, don't they? Especially poetry. There's much that's new and exciting. And then there's so much awful stuff."

We walked back inside and she poured the coffee. We sat and drank the coffee. I asked her who her favorite poets were. Janice quickly mentioned some of the younger ones: Sandra Merrill, Cynthia Westfall, Roberta Lowell, Sister Sarah Norbert and Adrian Poor.

"I wrote my first poem in grammar school, a Mother's Day poem. The teacher liked it so much that she asked me to read it in front of the class."

"Your first poetry reading, eh?"

Janice laughed, "Yes, you might say so. I miss both of my parents very much. They've been dead over 20 years."

"That's unusual."

"There's nothing unusual about love," she said.

She had been born in Huntington Beach and had lived all her life on the west coast. Her father had been a policeman. Janice began writing sonnets in high school where she was fortunate enough to be in a class taught by Inez Claire Dickey. "She introduced me to the discipline of poetic form."

Janice poured more coffee. "I was always serious about being a poet. I studied under Ivor Summers at Stanford. My first publication was in *An Anthology of Western Poets* edited by Summers." Summers was a profound influence on her—at first. The Summers group was a good one: Ashberry Charleton, Webdon Wilbur, and Mary Cather Henderson.

But then Janice broke away and joined the poets of "the long line."

Janice was in law school and also studying poetry. After graduating she became a legal secretary. She married her high school sweetheart during the early forties, "those dark and tragic

181

war years." Her husband was a fireman. "I evolved into a housewife-poetess."

"Is there a bathroom?" I asked.

"The door to your left."

I walked into the bathroom as Tony circled her taking photos. I urinated and took a good belt of the vodka. I zipped up and stepped out of the bathroom and sat down again.

In the late forties Janice Altrice's poems began to flower in a number of periodicals. Her first book, *I Command Everything To Be Green*, was published by Alan Swillout. It was followed by *Bird, Bird, Bird, Never Die* also brought out by Swillout.

"I went back to school," she said. "UCLA. I took an M.A. in journalism and an M.A. in English. I received my Ph.D. in English the following year, and since the early sixties I've taught English and Creative Writing at the State University here."

Many awards adorned Janice's walls: a silver medal from The Los Angeles Aphids Club for her poem "Tintella"; a first place certificate from the Lodestone Mountain Poetry Group for her poem "The Wise Drummer." There were many other prizes and awards. Janice went to her desk and took out some of her work in progress. She read us several long poems. They showed impressive growth. I asked her what she thought of the contemporary poetry scene.

"There are so *many*," she said, "who go by the name of *poet*. But they have no training, no feeling for their craft. The savages have taken over the castle. There's no workmanship, no care, simply a demand to be accepted. And these new poets all seem to admire one another. It worries me and I've talked about it to a lot of my poet friends. All a young poet seems to think he needs is a typewriter and a few pieces of paper. They aren't prepared, they have had no preparation at all."

"I suppose not," I said. "Tony, do you have enough photos?"

"Yeah," said Tony.

"Another thing which disturbs me," said Janice, "is that the eastern Establishment poets receive too many of the awards and fellowships. Western poets are ignored."

"Is it possible that the eastern poets are better?" I asked.

"I certainly don't think so."

"Well," I said, "I suppose it's time for us to go. One last question. How do you approach the writing of a poem?"

She paused. Her long fingers delicately stroked the heavy fabric that covered her chair. The setting sun slanted through the window and cast shadows in the room. She spoke slowly, as if in a dream. "I begin to feel a poem a long way off. It approaches me, like a cat, across the rug. Softly but not with contempt. It takes seven or eight days. I become delightfully agitated, excited, it's such a special feeling. I know it's there, and then it comes with a *rush*, and it's easy, so easy. The glory of creating a poem, it's so regal, so sublime!"

I switched off the tape recorder. "Thank you, Janice, I'll send you copies of the interview when it's published."

"I hope it went all right."

"It went quite well, I'm sure."

She walked us to the door. Tony and I walked down the slope to our car. I turned once. She was standing there. I waved. Janice smiled and waved back. We got in, drove around the bend, then I stopped the car and unscrewed the cap off the vodka bottle. "Save me a hit," said Tony. I took a hit and saved him a hit.

Tony threw the bottle out the window. We drove away, coming quickly down out of the hills. Well, it beat working in a car wash. All I had to do was type it up off the tape and select two or three photos. We came out of the hills just in time to hit the rush hour traffic. It was strictly the shits. We could have timed it much better than that.

COLD NIGHT

Leslie walked along under the palm trees. He stepped over a dog turd. It was 10:15 p.m. in east Hollywood. The market had gone up 22 points that day and the experts couldn't explain why. The experts were much better at explaining when the market went down. Doom made them happy. It was cold in east Hollywood. Leslie buttoned the top button on his coat and shivered. He hunched his shoulders against the chill.

A little man in a grey felt hat approached him. The man had a face like the front of a watermelon, no expression. Leslie pulled out a cigarette and stepped into the little man's path. The man was about 45, five-feet-six, maybe 140 pounds.

"Got a match, sir?" he asked the man.

"Oh, yes . . ." The man reached into his pocket and as he did Leslie kneed him in the groin. The man grunted and bent forward and Leslie clubbed him behind one ear. When the man fell Leslie kneeled and rolled him over, pulled out his knife and slit the man's throat in the cold east Hollywood moonlight.

It was all very strange. It was like a half-remembered dream. Leslie couldn't be sure if it was all actually happening or not. At first the blood seemed to hesitate, there was just the deep wound, then the blood gushed forth. Leslie pulled back in disgust. He got up, walked away. Then he returned, reached into the man's pocket, found the book of matches, stood up, lit his cigarette and walked away down the street to his apartment. Leslie never had enough matches, a man was always short of matches, it seemed. Matches and ballpoint pens . . .

Leslie sat down with a scotch and water. The radio played some Copeland. Well, Copeland wasn't much but it beat Sinatra. You took what you got and you tried to make do. That's what his old man had told him. Fuck his old man. Fuck all the Jesus freaks. Fuck Billy Graham right up the old rugged tailpipe.

There was a knock on the door. It was Sonny, the young blonde kid who lived across from him on the opposite side of the court. Sonny was half man and half dick and he was confused. Most guys with big dicks had trouble when the fucking was over. But Sonny was nicer than most; he was mild, he was gentle and he had some intelligence. Sometimes he was even funny.

"Listen, Leslie, I want to talk to you for a few minutes."

"O.K. But shit, I'm tired. I was at the track all day."

"Bad, huh?"

"When I got back to the parking lot after it was over I found some son of a bitch had ripped off my fender getting out of there. That's such dumb stale shit, you know."

"How'd you make out with the horses?"

"I won $280. But I'm tired."

"O.K. I won't stay long."

"All right. What is it? Your old lady? Why don't you beat the shit out of your old lady? You'll both feel better."

"No, my old lady's all right. It's just . . . shit, I don't know. Things, you know. I can't seem to get *into* anything. I can't seem to get *started*. Everything's locked up. All the cards are taken."

"Fuck, that's standard. Life's a one-sided game. But you're only 27, maybe you'll luck into something, somehow."

"What were you doing when you were my age?"

"Worse off than you. I used to lay out in the dark at night, drunk, on the street, hoping somebody would run me over. No luck."

"You couldn't think of another way?"

"That's one of the hardest things, figuring out what your first move should be."

"Yeah. Things seem so useless."

"We murdered God's son. Do you think that Bastard is going to forgive us? I may be crazy but I know He's not!"

"You sit there in your torn bathrobe and you're drunk half the time but you're saner than anybody I know."

"Hey, I like that. Do you know a lot of people?"

186

Sonny just shrugged. "What I need to know: is there a way out? Is there any kind of way out?"

"Kid, there's no way out. The shrinks advise us to take up chess or stamp collecting or billiards. Anything rather than think about the larger issues."

"Chess is boring."

"Everything is boring. There's no escape. You know what some old time bums used to tattoo on their arms: 'BORN TO DIE.' As corny as that sounds it's basic wisdom."

"What do you think the bums have tattooed on their arms now?"

"I don't know. Probably something like 'JESUS SHAVES.' "

"We can't get away from God, can we?"

"Maybe He can't get away from us."

"Well, listen, it's always good to talk to you. I always feel better after I talk to you."

"Anytime, kid."

Sonny got up, opened the door, closed it and was gone. Leslie poured another scotch. Well, the L.A. Rams had drafted for their defensive line. A good move. Everything in life was evolving toward DEFENSE. The iron curtain, the iron mind, the iron life. Some real tough coach would finally punt on first down every time his team got the ball and he'd never lose a game.

Leslie finished the scotch, pulled his pants down and scratched his ass, digging the fingers in. People who cured their hemorrhoids were fools. When there wasn't anybody else around it beat being alone. Leslie poured himself another scotch. The phone rang.

"Hello?"

It was Francine. Francine liked to impress him. Francine liked to think she impressed him. But she was an elephantine bore. Leslie often thought about how kind he was to let her bore him the way she did. The average guy would drop the receiver on her like a guillotine.

Who was it who had written that excellent essay about the guillotine? Camus? Camus, yes. Camus had been a bore, too. But the guillotine essay and *The Stranger* were exceptional.

"I had lunch at the Beverly Hills Hotel today," she said. "I had a table to myself. I had a salad and drinks. Dustin Hoffman was there and some other movie stars, too. I talked to the people sitting near me and they smiled and nodded, all the tables of smiles and nods, little yellow faces like daffodils. I kept talking and they kept smiling. They thought I was some kind of nut and the way to get rid of me was to smile. They became more and more nervous. Do you understand?"

"Of course."

"I thought you might like to hear about that."

"Yeah . . ."

"Are you alone? Do you want company?"

"I'm really tired tonight, Francine."

After a while Francine hung up. Leslie undressed, scratched his ass again and walked into the bathroom. He ran the dental floss between his few remaining teeth. What an ugliness, this hanging on. He ought to smash out the remaining teeth with a hammer. All the alley fights he had been in and nobody had gotten the front teeth. Well, everything would be gone eventually. Over. Leslie put some Crest on the electric toothbrush and tried to buy some time.

After that he sat up in bed for a long while with a last scotch and a cigarette. They were, at least, something to do while you waited to see how things would turn out. He looked at the matchbook in his hand and suddenly realized it was the one he'd taken from the man with the watermelon face. The thought startled him. Had that really happened or not? He stared at the matchbook, wondering. He looked at the cover:

1,000 PERSONALIZED LABELS
WITH YOUR NAME AND ADDRESS
JUST $1.00

Now, he thought, that doesn't seem to be such a bad deal.

A FAVOR FOR DON

I rolled over in bed and picked up the phone. It was Lucy Sanders. I'd known her two or three years, sexually for three months. We had just split up. She was telling the story that she had dumped me because I was a drunk but the truth was that I had left her for my previous girlfriend.

She hadn't taken it well. I decided I should go over to explain to her why it was necessary for me to leave her. In the book it's called "letting them down easy." I wanted to be a nice guy. When I got there her girlfriend let me in.

"What the hell do you want?"

"I want to let Lucy down easy."

"She's in the bedroom."

I walked in. She was on her bed, drunk, dressed only in panties. She had almost emptied a pint of scotch. There was a pot on the floor into which she had vomited.

"Lucy," I said.

She turned her head. "It's you, you've come back! I knew you wouldn't stay with that bitch."

"Now wait a minute, baby, I just came to explain why I left you. I'm a nice guy. I thought I'd explain."

"You're a bastard. You're a horrible man!"

I sat down on the edge of the bed, took the bottle off the headboard and had a good swallow.

"Thanks. Now you knew I loved Lilly. You knew that when I lived with you. Her and me—we have an understanding."

"But you said she was killing you!"

"Just dramatics. People split up and go back together all the time. It's part of the process."

"I took you in. I saved you."

"I know. You saved me for Lilly."

"You bastard, you don't know a good woman when you have one!"

Lucy leaned over the edge of the bed and vomited.

I finished off the pint. "You shouldn't drink this stuff. It's poison."

She pulled herself up. "Stay with me, Larry, don't go back to her. Stay with me!"

"Can't do it, baby."

"Look at my legs! I have nice legs! Look at my breasts! I have nice breasts!"

I threw the pint in the wastebasket. "Sorry, I gotta go, baby."

Lucy leaped off the bed at me with her fists doubled. The punches hit me in the mouth, the nose. I let her work away for a couple of seconds, then grabbed her wrists and threw her back on the bed. I turned and walked out of the bedroom. Her girlfriend was in the front room.

"Try to be a nice guy, you get a scab on your nose," I told her.

"There's no way you will ever be a nice guy," she said.

I slammed the door, got in my car and drove off.

It was Lucy on the phone. "Larry?"

"Yeh. What is it?"

"Listen—I want to meet your friend, Don."

"Why?"

"You said he was your only friend. I'd like to meet your only friend."

"Well, hell, all right."

"Thanks."

"I'm going over to his place after I visit my daughter on Wednesday. I'll be there about 5:00. Why don't you come by about 5:30 and I'll introduce you?"

I gave her the address and instructions. Don Dorn was a painter. He was 20 years younger than I was and lived in a small house on the beach. I turned over and went back to sleep. I always slept until noon. It was the secret of my successful existence.

★ ★ ★

Don and I had two or three beers before Lucy arrived. She appeared excited and had brought along a bottle of wine. I made the introductions and Don uncorked the wine. Lucy sat between us and drained her glass of wine. Don and I stuck with our beer.

"Oh," said Lucy, looking at Don, "he's just *gorgeous!*"

Don didn't say anything. She tugged at his shirt. "You're just *gorgeous!*" She emptied her glass and poured another. "Did you just get out of the shower?"

"About an hour ago."

"Oh, you have ringlets in your hair! You're *gorgeous!*"

"How's the painting coming, Don?" I asked.

"I don't know. I'm getting tired of my style. I think I've got to break into another area."

"Oh, are these *your* paintings on the wall?" Lucy asked.

"Yeh."

"They're marvelous! Do you sell them?"

"Sometimes."

"I just *love* your fish! Where did you get all the fish tanks?"

"I bought them."

"Look at that orange fish! I just *love* that orange one!"

"Yeh. He's nice."

"Do they eat each other?"

"Sometimes."

"You're *gorgeous!*"

Lucy drank glass after glass of wine.

"You're drinking too fast," I said.

"Look who's talking."

"You still with Lilly?" asked Don.

"Solid gold," I said.

Lucy drained her glass. The bottle was empty. "Excuse me," she said. She ran to the bathroom. Then we heard her vomiting.

"How are the horses running?" Don asked.

"Pretty good right now. How's your life going? Had any good fucks lately?"

"I've run into a streak of bad luck."

"Keep the faith. Your luck might change."

"I sure as hell hope so."

"Lilly keeps getting better and better. I don't see how she does it."

Lucy came out of the bathroom. "My god, I'm sick, I'm dizzy!" She threw herself on Don's bed and stretched out. "I'm dizzy."

"Just close your eyes," I said.

Lucy lay on the bed looking at me and moaning. Don and I drank some more beer. Then I told him I had to leave.

"Stay healthy," I said.

"God bless," he said.

I left him standing in the doorway, rather drunk, and drove off.

I rolled over in bed and picked up the phone.

"Hello?"

It was Lucy.

"I'm sorry about last night. I drank that wine too fast. But I cleaned up the bathroom like a good little girl. Don's a nice fellow. I really like him. I might buy one of his paintings."

"Good. He needs the scratch."

"You're not mad at me, are you?"

"What for?"

She laughed. "I mean, getting sick and all that."

"Everyone in America gets sick now and then."

"I'm not a drunk."

"I know."

"I'll be home all weekend if you decide you want to see me."

"I don't."

"You're not mad, Larry?"

"No."

"All right then. Toodleoooo."

"Toodleoooo."

I put the phone back in its cradle and closed my eyes. If I kept winning at the track I was going to buy a new car. I was going to move to Beverly Hills. The phone rang again.

"Hello?"

It was Don.

"Are you all right?" he asked.

"I'm all right. Are you all right?"

"I'm fine."

"I'm going to move to Beverly Hills."

"Sounds great."

192

"I want to live closer to my daughter."

"How's your daughter doing?"

"She's beautiful. She has everything, inside and out."

"You heard from Lucy?"

"She just phoned."

"She sucked me off."

"How was it?"

"I couldn't come."

"Sorry."

"It wasn't your fault."

"I hope not."

"Well, you're all right then, Larry?"

"I think so."

"O.K., keep in touch."

"Sure. Goodbye, Don."

I put the phone back in its cradle and closed my eyes. It was only 10:45 a.m. and I always slept until noon. Life's as kind as you let it be.

PRAYING MANTIS

Angel's View Hotel. Marty paid the clerk, took the key and was walking up the stairway. It was less than a pleasant night. Room 222. What did that mean? He walked inside and flipped on the light. A dozen roaches crawled away into the wallpaper and chewed and moved and chewed. There was a telephone, a pay phone. He put the dime in and dialed the number. She answered. "Toni?" he asked.

"Yeh, this is Toni . . ." she said.

"Toni, I'm going crazy."

"I told you I'd come see you. Where you at?"

"The Angel View, Sixth and Coronado, Room 222."

"I'll see you in a couple of hours."

"Can't you come now?"

"Listen, I've got to take the kids over to Carl's, then I want to stop off and see Jeff and Helen, I haven't seen them in years . . ."

"Toni, I love you for Christ's sake, I want to see you now!"

"Maybe if you got rid of your wife, Marty . . ."

"These things take time."

"See you in a couple of hours, Marty."

"Listen, Toni . . ."

She hung up. Marty walked over and sat on the edge of the bed. This would be his last involvement. It took too much out of him. Women were stronger than men. They knew all the moves. He didn't know any of the moves.

There was a knock on the door. He walked over and opened it. It was a blonde in her mid-thirties in a torn blue smock. The mascara was very purple and the lipstick was on heavy. There was

195

a slight smell of gin.

"Listen, you don't mind if I play my tv, do you?"

"It's all right, go ahead."

"Last guy had your room was some kind of nut. I'd turn on my tv and he'd start banging on the walls."

"It's all right. You can play your tv." Marty closed the door. He dug the next to last cigarette out of his pack and lit it. That Toni was in his blood, he had to get her out of his blood. There was another knock on the door. It was the blonde again. The mascara was purple and her eyes almost matched; of course it was impossible, but it looked as if she had added another layer of lipstick.

"Yes?" asked Marty.

"Listen," she said, "do you know what the female praying mantis does while they are doing the thing?"

"What thing?"

"Fucking."

"What does she do?"

"She eats his head off. While they are doing the thing she eats his head off. Well, I guess there are worse ways to die, don't you think?"

"Yeah," said Marty, "like cancer."

The blonde walked into the room and closed the door behind her. She walked over and sat in the only chair. Marty sat on the bed. "Did it get you excited when I said 'fucking'?" she asked.

"Yeah, a little."

The blonde got up from the chair and walked over to the bed and put her head real close to Marty's, she looked into his eyes and put her lips very close to his. Then she said, *"Fucking, fucking, fucking!"* She got a little closer, then said it once more: "FUCK-ING!" Then she walked over and sat back down in the chair.

"What's your name?" asked Marty.

"Lilly. Lilly LaVell. I used to strip at the Burbank."

"I'm Marty Evans. Glad to know you, Lilly."

"Fucking," said Lilly very slowly, spreading her lips and showing her tongue.

"You can play your tv anytime," said Marty.

"You heard about the black widow spider?" she asked.

"I don't know."

"Well, I'll tell you. After they do the thing—*fucking*—she eats him alive."

"Oh," said Marty.

"But there are worse ways of dying, don't you think?"

"Sure, like leprosy, maybe."

The blonde got up and walked up and down, up and down. "I got drunk the other night, I was out on the freeway, I was listening to a horn concerto, Mozart, that horn ran right *through* me, I'm doing 85 miles an hour and I'm driving with my elbows listening to this horn concerto, can you believe that?"

"Sure, I believe it."

Lilly stopped walking and looked at Marty. "Do you believe I can get you in my mouth and do things to you that have never been done to a man?"

"Well, I don't know what to believe."

"Well, I can, I can . . ."

"You're nice, Lilly, but I've got to meet my girlfriend here in about an hour."

"Well, I'll get you ready for her."

Lilly walked over beside him, unzipped him and pulled his penis out of his jockey shorts.

"Oh, he's cute!"

Lilly wet her middle finger, right hand, and began to rub the head and just below and back of the head.

"But he's so purple!"

"Just like your mascara . . ."

"Oh, he's getting so BIG!"

Marty laughed. A roach crawled out on the wallpaper to catch the action. Then another came out. They wiggled their feelers. Suddenly Lilly's mouth was on his penis. She gripped him right below the head and sucked. Her tongue was almost like sandpaper; it seemed to know all the right places. Marty looked down at the top of her head and became very excited. He began to pet her hair and sounds dropped out of his mouth. Then suddenly she bit into his cock, hard. She almost bit him in half. Then still biting she yanked her head up. A piece of the head came off. Marty screamed and rolled over and over on the bed. The blonde stood up and spit. Pieces of flesh and blood spattered on the rug. Then she walked over, opened the door, closed it and was gone.

Marty took the pillowcase off and held it against his penis. He was afraid to look. He felt his heartbeat throbbing throughout his whole body, especially down there. The blood began to spread through the pillowcase. Then the phone rang. He managed to get up, walk over and answer it. "Yeh?" "Marty?" "Yeh?" "This is Toni." "Yeh, Toni . . ." "You sound funny . . ." "Yeh, Toni . . ." "Is that all you can say? I'm over at Jeff and Helen's. I'll see you in about an hour." "Sure." "Listen, what's wrong with you? I thought you loved me?" "I don't know any more, Toni . . ." "All right, then," she said angrily and hung up.

Marty managed to find a dime and get it in the phone. "Operator, I want a private ambulance service. Get me anybody but do it fast. I may be dying . . ."

"Have you checked with your doctor, sir?"

"Operator, please get me a private ambulance service!"

Next door to the left, the blonde sat in front of her tv set. She reached over and switched it on. She was just in time for the Dick Cavett Show.

BROKEN MERCHANDISE

Frank pulled onto the freeway into the traffic.

He was a shipping clerk for the American Clock Company. Six years now. Never held a job for six years before and now the son of a bitch was really killing him. But at the age of 42 with a high school education and ten percent unemployment he didn't have much choice. It was his 15th or 16th job and all the jobs had been terrible.

Frank was tired and he wanted to get home and have a beer. He maneuvered his Volks into the fast lane. When he got out there he was no longer so sure that he was in a hurry to get home. Fran would be waiting. Four years now.

He knew what was coming. Fran couldn't wait for the first verbal shot. He always waited for her first shot. Jesus, she couldn't wait to put the knock on him. Then, knock, knock, knock . . .

Frank knew he was a loser. He didn't need Fran to remind him of the fact, to illuminate it. You'd think that two people living together would help each other. But no, they fell into the habit of criticism. He criticized her, she criticized him. They were both losers. Now all they had left was to see who could be the most sarcastic about it all.

And that son of a bitch, Meyers. Meyers had walked back to the shipping department ten minutes before quitting time and stood there.

"Frank."

"Yes?"

"Are you putting FRAGILE labels on all the shipments?"

"Yes."

"Are you packing carefully?"

"Yes."

"We're getting more and more complaints from our customers about receiving broken merchandise."

"I suppose that accidents occur in transit."

"Are you sure you're packing the shipments properly?"

"Yes."

"Maybe we had better try some different trucking lines?"

"They're all the same."

"Well, I want to see an improvement. I want less breakage."

"Yes, sir."

Meyers had once controlled the American Clock Company but drinking and a bad marriage had ruined him. He had had to sell most of his stock and was now only an assistant manager. He had gone on the wagon and as a result was always irritable. Meyers was continually trying to draw Frank out and make him angry. Then he would have an excuse to fire him.

There was nothing worse than a reformed drunk and a Born Again Christian and Meyers was both . . .

Frank drew up behind an old car in the fast lane. It was a battered gas-eater, a sedan, and it gave off a dirty trail of smoke from the exhaust. The fenders were smashed and vibrated as the sedan drove along. The paint job had almost vanished from the car, it was almost colorless, a smog grey.

All that didn't bother Frank. What bothered him was that the car was going too slow, going the same speed as the car opposite it in the next lane. He checked his speedometer. They were all doing 52. Why?

Maybe it didn't matter. Fran was waiting. It was Fran at one end and Meyers at the other. The only time he had alone, the only time somebody wasn't ripping at him was when he was driving back and forth to work. Or when he was asleep.

But still he didn't like being boxed in on the freeway. It was senseless. He looked at the two guys in the front seat of the sedan. They were both talking at once and laughing. They were two young punks about 23 or 24. Frank was glad he didn't have to listen to the conversation. Those punks were beginning to irritate him.

Then Frank saw his chance. The car on the right of the old sedan was going just a little bit faster, it was pulling ahead. Frank swung around behind the other car.

He began to taste the freedom of busting out of there. It would be a small victory after a horrible day with a horrible evening to come. He was going to make it.

Then just as he was getting ready to cut out in front of the old sedan the punk at the wheel stepped on the gas, pulled up, cut him off and drove alongside the other car again.

Frank swung back behind the punks' car. They were still talking and laughing. He saw their bumper sticker. JESUS LOVES YOU.

Then he noticed a decal on the rear window. THE WHO.

Well, they had Jesus and they had The Who. Why in the hell couldn't they let him by?

Frank pulled up behind them, rode their rear bumper. They went on talking and laughing. They kept driving at exactly the same speed as the car to their right. 50 mph.

Frank checked his rear view mirror. There was an unbroken stream of traffic as far back as he could see.

Frank worked his Volks from the fast lane into the next lane, then worked over into the slow lane. Traffic was moving faster there. He slipped around a car by darting left and then broke loose into the open. As he did he saw the old sedan speed up. The punks pulled up alongside of him. Frank checked his speedometer. 62 mph. Frank ran it up to 65. The punks were still there. He pushed it to 70. The punks stayed with him.

Now they were in a hurry. Why?

Frank pushed the accelerator all the way down. The Volks would only do 75. He was going to burn up the engine or throw a rod. The punks were keeping up with him even though they were grinding their car to death too.

He looked over at them. Two young blond guys with wisps of goatees. Their faces looked at him. Bland faces like turkey butts with little holes for mouths.

The punk next to the driver gave him the finger.

Frank pointed first at the finger guy, then at the driver. Then he pointed to the freeway exit. They both nodded.

Frank led them to the freeway exit. He stopped at a signal. They waited behind him. Then Frank took a right and drove along with the punks behind him. He drove until he saw a supermarket. He drove into the parking lot. He noted the loading dock. It was dark back there. The market was closed. The dock was deserted, the steel doors pulled down. There was nothing back there but space and stacks of empty wooden crates. Frank pulled up to the loading dock. He got out of his car, locked it and walked up the ramp and along the dock. The punks pulled in their old sedan alongside his car and got out.

They walked up the ramp toward him. Neither one of them weighed over 130 pounds. Together they only outweighed him 30 pounds.

Then the guy who had given the finger said, "O.K., you old shit!" He rushed at Frank, making a high, squealing sound, his hands held flat in some kind of karate gesture. The punk whirled, tried a backward kick, missed, then came around and cracked Frank on the ear with the side of his hand. It was no more than a slap. Frank put all of his 230 pounds behind a hard right to the punk's belly and the kid slumped to the pavement holding his gut.

The other punk pulled out a switchblade, flicked it open.

"I'll cut your fuckin' balls off!" he said to Frank.

Frank waited as the punk moved in, nervously changing the knife from hand to hand. Frank backed up toward the crates. The punk moved in making hissing sounds. Frank waited, his back against the boxes. Then as the punk moved in Frank reached up, grabbed a crate and threw it at him. It slammed into the punk's face and as it did Frank moved in and grabbed his knife arm. The blade fell to the ground and Frank twisted the arm behind the punk's back. He pushed the arm up as far as he could.

"*Please don't break my arm!*" the punk squealed.

Frank let the punk go and as he did he kicked him in the ass, hard. The kid fell forward, grabbing at his butt. Frank picked up the knife, flicked in the blade, pocketed it and walked slowly back to his car. As he got in and started the Volks he could see the two punks standing close to each other by the old sedan watching him. They were no longer talking and laughing.

Suddenly he gunned his car and ran it at them. They scattered and at the last moment he veered off. He slowed down and drove out of the parking lot.

He noticed that his hands were trembling. It had been one hell of a day. He drove along the boulevard. The Volks ran badly, sputtering, as if to object to its mistreatment on the freeway.

Then Frank saw the bar. The Lucky Knight. There was parking in front. He stopped, got out and went in.

Frank sat down and ordered a Bud. "Where's your phone?"

The barkeep told him. It was back near the crapper. He put the coin in and dialed the number.

"Yes?" Fran answered.

"Listen, Fran, I'm going to be a little late. I got held up. See you soon."

"Held up? You mean you got robbed?"

"No, I got in a fight."

"A *fight!* Don't tell me that! You couldn't fight your way out of a paper bag!"

"Fran, I wish you wouldn't use those old, stale expressions."

"Well, it's true! You couldn't fight your way out of a paper bag!"

Frank hung up and walked back to the bar stool. He picked up his bottle of Bud and took a hit.

"I like a man who drinks right out of the bottle!"

There was somebody sitting next to him. A woman. She was about 38, dirt under her fingernails, her dyed blonde hair piled loosely on top of her head. Two silver loops dangled from her ears and her mouth was heavy with lipstick. She licked her lips, slowly, then she stuck a Virginia Slim into that mouth and lit it.

"I'm Diana."

"Frank. What do you drink?"

"He knows . . ." She nodded to the barkeep and the barkeep picked up a bottle of her favorite brand of whiskey and moved toward them. Frank pulled out a ten and placed it on the bar.

"You got a fascinating face," said Diana. "What do you do?"

"Nothing."

"Just the kind of man I like."

She lifted her drink and pressed her leg against his as she drank. Frank took his fingernail and slowly peeled the wet beer label off his bottle. Diana finished her drink. Frank motioned to the barkeep.

"Two more."

"Yeah, what'll you have?"

"I'll take hers."

"You'll take hers?" asked the barkeep. *"Wow!"*

They all laughed. Frank lit a smoke and the barkeep brought the bottle down. Suddenly it looked like a pretty good night after all.

HOME RUN

I guess I was about 28 at that time. I wasn't working but I had a little money because I had lucked it at the track — finally. It was around 9 p.m. I had been drinking in my rented room for a couple of hours. I was bored and I came out and started walking down the street. I came to a bar across the street from my usual bar and for some reason I went in. It was a lot cleaner and fancier in there than in my usual bar and I thought, well, maybe I'll luck into a class piece of ass.

I sat down near the entrance, took a stool a couple of seats away from this girl. She was alone and there were four or five people, men and women, at the other end of the bar. The barkeep was down there talking to them and laughing. I must have sat three or four minutes. The barkeep just kept talking and laughing. I hated those pricks, they drank all they wanted, got tips, got ass, got admiration, got everything they wanted.

I pulled out a pack of smokes. Tapped one out. No matches. None on the bar. I looked at the lady.

"Pardon me, got a light?"

Irritated, she dug into her purse. She came up with a book of matches, Then without looking at me, she tossed them down.

"Keep 'em," she said.

She had long hair and a good body. She had on a fake fur coat and a little fur hat. I watched her tilt her head back after sucking at her smoke. She exhaled like she really knew some god damned thing. Those are the kind you like to belt-whip.

The barkeep kept ignoring me.

I picked up an ashtray, held it about two feet above the bar and dropped it. That got him. He came on down, treading the boards. He was a big one, maybe six-feet-four, 265 pounds. Some fat around the gut, but big shoulders, big head, big hands. He was handsome in a dumb kind of way, a strand of drunken hair hanging over one eye.

"Double Cutty Sark on the rocks," I told him.

"Good thing you didn't break that ashtray," he said.

"Good thing you heard it," I answered.

The boards creaked and groaned as he walked back to mix the drink.

"I hope he doesn't mix me a Mickey," I said to the girl in the fake mink.

"Jimmy's nice," she said. "Jimmy doesn't do things like that."

"'I've never met a nice guy named 'Jimmy,'" I told her.

Jimmy came back with my drink. I reached into my wallet and dropped a $50 bill on the bar. Jimmy picked it up, held it up to the light and said, "Shit!"

"What's the matter, boy?" I asked. "Never seen a $50 bill before?"

He walked off down the boards. I took a hit of my drink. It was a double all right.

"Guy acts like he never saw $50 before," I said to the girl in the fur hat. "I carry nothing but 50s."

"You're full of shit," she said.

"No, I'm not," I told her. "I took a dump about 20 minutes ago."

"Big deal . . ."

"I can buy anything you've got."

"It's not for sale," she said.

"What's the matter? You got a lock on it? If you have, don't worry, nobody's going to ask for the key."

I took another hit.

"Wanna drink?" I asked.

"I only drink with people I like," she said.

"Now you're full of shit," I told her.

Where's the barkeep with my change? I thought. He's taking a long time . . .

I was just about the drop the ashtray again when he came back, cracking wood with his dumb feet.

He put the change down. I looked at it as he started to walk off.

"HEY!" I yelled.

He came back down. "What is it?"

"This is change for a ten. I gave you $50."

"You gave me a ten . . ."

I turned to the girl. "Listen, you saw it, didn't you? I gave him $50!"

"You gave Jimmy a ten," she said.

"What the fuck *is* this?" I asked.

Jimmy began walking off.

"You can't get away with this!" I hollered.

He just kept on walking. He walked back to the gang at the end of the bar and they all started talking and laughing.

I sat there thinking about it. The girl next to me blew a plume of smoke out of her nose, her head tilted back.

I thought about smashing the mirror behind the bar. I'd done that once at another place. Yet, I hesitated.

Was I losing it?

That son of a bitch had pissed all over me with everybody watching.

His cool worried me more than his size. He had something else going for him. A gun under the bar? He wanted me to play into his hand. The witnesses would be his . . .

I didn't know what to do. There was a phone booth near the exit. I got up, went over, got in, dropped in a coin, dialed a number at random. I would pretend that I was calling my buddies, that they would come right over and bust up the bar. I listened to the number ringing at the other end. It stopped. A woman answered.

"Hello," she said.

"It's me," I answered.

"That you, Sam?"

"Yeah, yeah, now listen . . ."

"Sam, a terrible thing happened today! Wooly got run over!"

"Wooly?"

"Our *dog,* Sam! Wooly's *dead!*"

"Now, listen! I'm at the Red Eye! You know where it's at? Good! I want you to bring Lefty and Larry and Tony and Big Angelo down here, *fast! Got* it? And bring *Wooly* too!"

I hung up and sat there. I thought about calling the police. I knew what would happen then. They'd back up the barkeep. And I'd end up in the drunk tank.

I got out of the phone booth and walked back to my bar stool. I finished my drink. Then I picked up the ashtray and dropped it, hard. The barkeep looked at me. I stood up, raised my arm and pointed a finger at him. Then I turned and walked out the exit, his laughter and the laughter of his crowd following me . . .

I stopped at the liquor store, picked up two bottles of wine, and went to the Hotel Helen which was across the street from the bar I had been in. I had a girlfriend there, an alky like me. She was ten years older than I was, and she worked as a maid there. I walked up two flights, knocked on her door, hoping she'd be alone.

"Baby," I called, "I'm in trouble. I've been fucked-over . . ."

The door opened. Betty was alone and drunker than I was.

I walked in and closed the door behind me.

"Where are your drinking glasses?"

She pointed and I peeled a bottle and poured two. She sat on the edge of the bed and I sat in a chair. I passed her the bottle. She lit a cigarette.

"I hate this place, Benny. How come we don't live together anymore?"

"You started running the streets, baby, you drove me crazy."

"Well, you know how I am."

"Yeah . . ."

Betty took her cigarette and absentmindedly pushed it down into the bedsheet. I saw the smoke start to come up. I walked over and lifted her hand. There was a plate on the dresser. I got it and brought it over. It had dried food on it, looked like a tamale. I put the plate next to her on the bed.

"Here's an ashtray . . ."

"You know I miss you," she said.

I drained my wine, poured another. "Look, I got short-changed out of $50 across the street."

"Where'd *you* get $50?"

"Never mind, I got it. That son of a bitch short-changed me . . ."

"Why didn't you bust him up? You scared? That's Jimmy. The women *love* him! Every night after the bar closes he goes out back in the parking lot and sings. They stand around and listen and then one of them gets to go home with him."

"He's a hunk of shit . . ."

"He played football for Notre Dame."

"What kind of crap is that? You go for this guy?"

"I can't stand him."

"Good. Because I'm going to bust his sack."

"I think you're scared . . ."

"Ever seen me duck a fight?"

"I've seen you lose a few."

I didn't answer that remark. We kept drinking and the conversation wandered around to other things. I don't remember much about the conversation. When she wasn't running the streets Betty was a pretty good soul. She had sense, but she was confused, you know. A total alky. *I* could quit for a day or two. She never could stop. It was sad. We talked. We had an understanding which made it easy to be around one another. Then it got to be 2 a.m. Betty said, "Come here, watch . . ."

We went to the window and there was Jimmy the barkeep out in the parking lot. Sure enough, he was singing. There were three girls watching him. There was plenty of laughter.

Much of it about my $50 bill, I thought.

Then one of the girls got into his car with him. The other two walked off. The car sat a moment. The lights came on, the engine kicked over, then he drove off.

What a flash-ass, I thought. I never turn on my lights until *after* the engine kicks over.

I looked at Betty. "That son of a bitch really thinks he's a hot number. I'm gonna bust his sack."

"You don't have the guts," she answered.

"Listen," I asked, "you still have that baseball bat under your bed?"

"Yeah, but I can't part with it . . ."

"Sure you can," I said, handing her a ten.

"O.K." She slid it out from under the bed. "Hope you hit a homer . . ."

The next night at 2 a.m. I was waiting in the parking lot, up against the side of the bar, crouched behind a couple of large garbage cans. I had Betty's baseball bat, an old Jimmy Foxx special.

I didn't have to wait long. The barkeep came out with his girls.

"Sing for us, Jimmy!"

"Sing us one of your *own* songs!"

"Well . . . all right," he said.

He took off his necktie, stuck it in his pocket, unbuttoned his shirt at the neck, lifted his head to the moon.

"I am the man you're waiting for . . .
I am the man you must adore . . .
I am the man who will fuck you on the floor . . .
I am the man who will make you ask for more . . .
. . . and more . . .
. . . and more . . ."

The three girls applauded and laughed and crowded around him.

"Oh, Jimmy!"

"Oh, JIMMY!"

Jimmy stepped back and looked the girls over. They waited. Finally he said, "O.K., tonight it's . . . Caroline . . ."

With that, the other two girls looked crestfallen, obediently ducked their heads and walked slowly out of the parking lot together, turning to smile and wave at Jimmy and Caroline as they reached the boulevard.

Caroline stood there, slightly drunk, swaying on her high heels. She had a nice body, long hair. She seemed familiar, somehow.

"You're a real man, Jimmy," she told him. "I love you."

"Bullshit, bitch, you just want to suck my cock."

"Yes, *that* too, Jimmy!" Caroline laughed.

"You're gonna suck my cock, right now," Jimmy said. Suddenly he sounded mean.

"No, wait . . . Jimmy, that's too *fast.*"

"You say you love me, then *suck* me."

"No, wait . . ."

Jimmy was pretty drunk. He had to be to act like that. There wasn't much light in that parking lot but it wasn't that dark either. But some guys were freaks. They liked to do it in public situations.

"You'll suck me, bitch, now . . ."

Jimmy unzipped, grabbed her by that long hair and forced her head down. I thought she was going to do it. She seemed to relent.

Then Jimmy screamed. *Screamed.*

She had bitten him. He pulled her up by the hair and hit her, fist closed, across the face. Then he dug a knee up between her legs and she fell, motionless.

She's out cold, I thought. Maybe I'll drag her back by those cans and fuck her after he drives off.

Damned if he didn't frighten me. I decided not to come out from behind those garbage cans. I clutched the Jimmy Foxx slugger and waited for him to leave.

I watched as he zipped up and walked gingerly to his car. He got the door open, climbed in and sat there a while. Then the lights flashed on and the engine kicked over.

He just sat there revving his motor.

Then I saw him climb out. The engine was still running. The lights were on.

He walked around to the front of the car.

"Hey!" he said loudly, "what's zat? I see . . . you . . ."

He started moving toward me.

". . . I see . . . you . . . who the fuck . . . is . . . hiding behind those cans? I see . . . you . . . come on outa there!"

He came toward me. The moon behind his back made him look like some god-forsaken creature out of a low budget horror film.

"You fucking roach!" he yelled, "I'll stamp the piss out of you!"

He came at me. I was caught behind the garbage cans. I raised the Jimmy Foxx slugger, came down with it and caught him squarely on top of the head.

He didn't drop. He just stood there staring at me. I hit him again. It was like an old time comedy movie in black and white. He just stood there and made a horrible face at me.

I slipped out from behind the garbage cans and started to walk away. He followed me.

I turned around.

"Leave me alone," I told him. "Let's forget it."

"I'm going to kill you, punk!" he said.

Those two big hands reached for my throat. I ducked away and swung the bat at one of his kneecaps. There was a shot like a gun going off and he dropped.

"Let's forget it," I told him. "Let's leave it like this."

He was on his hands and knees, crawling after me.

"I'm gonna kill ya, punk!"

I put the wood to the back of his neck as hard as I could then.

He was stretched out next to his unconscious friend. I looked at the girl, Caroline. It was the one with the fake fur. I decided I didn't want it after all.

I ran over to the barkeep's car, switched the lights off, killed the engine, pulled the keys and threw them onto the roof of the building. Then I ran back to the bodies and got Jimmy's wallet.

I ran out of the lot, walked south a few feet, and said, "Shit!" I turned and ran back to the lot and the garbage cans. I had left my whiskey there. A fifth in a paper bag. I got it.

I went south again to the corner, crossed the street, found a mailbox, looked around. Nobody. I took the bills out of the wallet, dropped the wallet into the box.

Next I walked north until I came to the Hotel Helen. I went in, went up the stairway, knocked on the door.

"BETTY, IT'S BENNY! FOR CHRIST'S SAKE, OPEN UP!"

The door opened.

"Shit . . . what is it?" she asked.

"I've got some whiskey."

I got inside, put the chain on the door. She had the lights on. I marched around cutting them off. Then it was dark.

"What's the matter," she asked, "you crazy?"

I found the glasses and with a shaking hand poured two.

I took her to the window. The police cars were already there, lights blinking.

"What the hell happened?" she asked.

"Some guy busted Jimmy's sack," I said.

You could hear the ambulance coming. Then it was in the parking lot. They loaded the girl in first. Then they got Jimmy.

"Who got the girl?" Betty asked.

"Jimmy . . ."

"Who got Jimmy?"

"What the hell does it matter?"

I set my drink on the window sill and reached into my pocket. I counted out the bills. $480.

"Here, baby . . ."

I handed her $50.

"Jesus, thanks, Benny!"

"It's nothing . . ."

"Those horses must really be coming in!"

"Better than ever, baby . . ."

"Cheers!" she said lifting her glass.

"Cheers," I said, lifting mine.

We clicked glasses, then drank them off as the ambulance backed out, turned south, siren on.

It just wasn't our turn yet.

FOOLING MARIE

It was a warm night at the quarterhorse races. Ted had arrived carrying $200 and now going into the third race he was carrying $530. He knew his horses. Maybe he wasn't much good at anything else but he knew his horses. Ted stood watching the toteboard and looking at the people. They lacked any ability to rate a horse. But they still brought their money and their dreams to the track. The track ran a $2 exacta almost every race to lure them in. That and the Pick-6. Ted never touched the Pick-6 or the exactas or the doubles. Just straight win on the best horse, which wasn't necessarily the favorite.

Marie bitched so much about his going to the track that he only went two or three times a week. He had sold his company and retired early from the construction business. There really wasn't much else for him to do.

The four horse looked good at six-to-one but there was still 18 minutes to post. He felt a tug at his coat sleeve.

"Pardon me, sir, but I've lost the first two races. I saw you cashing in your tickets. You look like a guy who knows what he's doing. Who do you like in this next race?"

She was a strawberry blonde, about 24, slender hips, surprisingly big breasts; long legs, a cute turned-up nose, flower mouth; dressed in a pale blue dress, wearing white high-heeled shoes. Her blue eyes looked up at him.

"Well," Ted smiled at her, "I've usually got the winner."

"I'm used to betting on thoroughbreds," said the strawberry blonde. "These quarterhorse races are so *fast!*"

"Yeah. Most of them are run in under 18 seconds. You find out pretty quick whether you're right or wrong."

"If my mother knew I was out here losing my money she'd belt-whip me."

"I'd like to belt-whip you myself," said Ted.

"You're not one of those, are you?" she asked.

"Just joking," said Ted. "Come on, let's go to the bar. Maybe we can pick you a winner."

"All right, Mr. —?"

"Just call me Ted. What's your name?"

"Victoria."

They walked into the bar. "What'll you have?" Ted asked.

"Whatever you're having," said Victoria.

Ted ordered two Jack Daniels. He stood and knocked his off and she sipped at hers, looking straight ahead. Ted checked her ass: perfect. She was better than some god damned movie starlet, and she didn't look spoiled.

"Now," said Ted, pointing to his program, "in the next race the four horse figures best and they are giving six-to-one odds . . ."

Victoria let out a very sexy, "Oooh . . .?" She leaned over to look at his program, touching him with her arm. Then he felt her leg press against his.

"People just don't know how to rate a horse," he told her. "Show me a man who can rate a horse and I'll show you a man who can win all the money he can carry."

She smiled at him. "I wish I had going what you've got going."

"You've got plenty going, baby. Want another drink?"

"Oh no, thank you . . ."

"Well, listen," said Ted, "we better bet."

"All right, I'll bet $2 to win. Which is it, the number four horse?"

"Yeah, baby, it's the four . . ."

They placed their bets and went out to watch the race. The four didn't break well, got bumped on both sides, righted himself, was running fifth in a nine horse field, but then began to accelerate and came down to the wire bobbing heads with the two-to-one favorite. Photo.

God damn, thought Ted, I've *got* to have this one. Please give me *this* one!

"Oh," said Victoria, "I'm so *excited!*"

The toteboard flashed the number. *Four.*

Victoria screamed and jumped up and down gleefully. "We won, we won, we WON!"

She grabbed Ted and he felt the kiss on his cheek.

"Take it easy, baby, the best horse won, that's all."

They waited for the official sign and then the tote flashed the payoff. $14.60.

"How much did you bet?" Victoria asked.

"Forty win," said Ted.

"How much do you get back?"

"$292. Let's collect."

They began walking toward the windows. Then Ted felt Victoria's hand in his. She pulled him to a stop.

"Bend over," she said, "I want to whisper something in your ear."

Ted leaned over, felt her cool pink lips up against his ear. "You're a . . . magic man . . . I want to . . . fuck you . . ."

Ted stood there grinning weakly at her. "My god," he said.

"What's the matter? Are you afraid?"

"No, no, it's not that . . ."

"What is the matter then?"

"It's Marie . . . my wife . . . I'm married . . . and she has me timed down to the minute. She knows when the races are over and when I'm due in."

Victoria laughed: "We'll leave *now!* We'll go to a motel!"

"Well, sure," said Ted . . .

They cashed their tickets and walked out to the parking lot. "We'll take my car. I'll drive you back when we're finished," Victoria said.

They found her car, a blue 1982 Fiat, it matched her dress. The license plate read: VICKY. As she put her key in the door, Victoria hesitated. "You're really not one of those kind, are you?"

"What kind?" Ted asked.

"A belt-whipper, one of those. My mother had a terrible experience once . . ."

"Relax," said Ted. "I'm harmless."

★　★　★

They found a motel about a mile and a half from the track. The Blue Moon. Only The Blue Moon was painted green. Victoria parked and they got out, went in, signed in, were given Room 302. They had stopped for a bottle of Cutty Sark on the way.

Ted peeled the cellophane from the glasses, lit a cigarette, and poured a couple as Victoria undressed. The panties and the bra were pink, and the body was pink and white and beautiful. It was amazing how now and then a woman was created who looked like that, when all the others, most of the others, had nothing, or next to nothing. It was maddening. Victoria was a beautiful, maddening dream.

Victoria was naked. She came over and sat on the edge of the bed next to Ted. She crossed her legs. Her breasts were very firm and she looked as if she was already aroused. He really couldn't believe his luck. Then she giggled.

"What is it?" he asked.

"Are you thinking about your wife?"

"Well, no, I was thinking about something else."

"Well, you *should* think about your wife . . ."

"Hell," said Ted, "*you* were the one who suggested fucking!"

"I wish you wouldn't use that word . . ."

"Are you backing out?"

"Well, no. Listen, you got a cigarette?"

"Sure . . ."

Ted pulled one out, handed it to her, lighted it as she held it in her mouth.

"You've got the most beautiful body I've ever seen," said Ted.

"I don't doubt that," she said, smiling.

"Hey, are you backing out of this thing?" he asked.

"Of course not," she answered, "get your clothes off."

Ted began undressing, feeling fat and old and ugly, but he also felt lucky—it had been his best day at the track, in many ways. He draped his clothes over a chair and sat down next to Victoria.

Ted poured a new drink for each of them.

"You know," he told her, "you're a class act but I'm a class act too. We each have our own way of showing it. I made it big in the construction business and I'm still making it big with the horses. Not everybody has that instinct."

Victoria drank half of her Cutty Sark and smiled at him. "Oh, you're my big fat Buddha!"

Ted drained his drink. "Listen, if you don't want to do it, we won't do it. Forget it."

"Lemme see what Buddha's got . . ."

Victoria reached down and slid her hand between his legs. She got it, she held it.

"Oh oh . . . I feel something . . ." Victoria said.

"Sure . . . So what?"

Then her head ducked down. She kissed it at first. Then he felt her open mouth and her tongue.

"You *cunt!*" he said.

Victoria lifted her head up and looked at him. "*Please,* I don't like dirty talk."

"All right, Vicky, all right. No dirty talk."

"Get under the sheets, Buddha!"

Ted got under there and he felt her body next to his. Her skin was cool and her mouth opened and he kissed her and pushed his tongue in. He liked it like that, fresh, spring fresh, young, new, good. What a god damned delight. He'd rip her! He played with her down there, she was a long time coming around. Then he felt her open up and he forced his finger in. He had her, the bitch. He pulled his finger out and rubbed the clit. You want foreplay, you'll get foreplay! he thought.

He felt her teeth dig into his lower lip, the pain was terrible. Ted pulled away, tasting the blood and feeling the wound on his lip. He half rose and slapped Victoria hard across the side of her face, then backhanded her across the other side of the face. He found her, down there, slid it in, rammed it in her while putting his mouth back on hers. Ted worked away in wild vengeance, now and then pulling his head back, looking at her. He tried to save it, to hold back, and then he saw that cloud of strawberry hair fanned across the pillow in the moonlight.

Ted was sweating and moaning like a high school boy. This was it. Nirvana. The place to be. Victoria was silent. Ted's moans lessened and then after a moment he rolled off.

He stared into the darkness.

I forgot to suck her tits, he thought.

Then he heard her voice. "You know what?" she asked.

"What?"

"You remind me of one of those quarterhorses."

"What do you mean?"

"It's all over in 18 seconds."

"We'll race again, baby," he said . . .

She went to the bathroom. Ted wiped off on the sheet, the old pro. Victoria was rather a nasty number, in a way. But she could be handled. He had something going. How many men owned their own home and had 150 grand in the bank at his age? He was a class act and she damn well knew it.

Victoria came walking out of the bathroom still looking cool, untouched, almost virginal. Ted switched on the bedlamp. He sat up and poured two more. She sat on the edge of the bed with her drink and he climbed out and sat on the edge of the bed next to her.

"Victoria," he said, "I can make things good for you."

"I guess you've got your ways, Buddha."

"And I'll be a better lover."

"Sure."

"Listen, you should have known me when I was young. I was tough, but I was good. I had it. I still have it."

She smiled at him, "Come on, Buddha, it's not all that bad. You've got a wife, you've got lots of things going for you."

"Except one thing," he said, draining his drink and looking at her. "Except the one thing I really want . . ."

"Look at your *lip!* You're bleeding!"

Ted looked down into his glass. There were drops of blood in his drink and he felt blood on his chin. He wiped his chin with the back of his hand.

"I'm going to shower and clean up, baby, be right back."

He walked into the bathroom, slid the shower door open and began to run the water, testing it with his hand. It seemed about right and he stepped in, the water running off him. He could see the blood in the water running into the drain. Some wildcat. All she needed was a steadying hand.

Marie was all right, she was kind, kind of dull actually. She had lost the intensity of youth. It wasn't her fault. Maybe he could find a way to stay with Marie and have Victoria on the side. Victoria renewed his youth. He needed some fucking renewal. And he needed some more good fucking like that. Of course, women were all crazy, they demanded more than there was. They didn't realize that making it was not a glorious experience, but only a necessary one.

"Hurry up, Buddha!" he heard her call. "Don't leave me all alone out here!"

"I won't be long, baby!" he yelled from under the shower.

He soaped up good, washing it all away.

Then Ted got out, toweled off, then opened the bathroom door and stepped into the bedroom.

The motel room was empty. She was gone.

There was a distance between ordinary objects and between events that was remarkable. All at once, he saw the walls, the rug, the bed, two chairs, the coffee table, the dresser, and the ashtray with their cigarettes. The distance between these things was immense. Then and now were light years apart.

On an impulse, he ran to the closet and pulled the door open. Nothing but coat hangers.

Then Ted realized that his clothes were gone. His underwear, his shirt, his pants, his car keys and wallet, his cash, his shoes, his stockings, everything.

On another impulse he looked under the bed. Nothing.

Then Ted noticed the bottle of Cutty Sark, half full, standing on the dresser and he walked over, picked it up and poured himself a drink. And as he did he saw two words scrawled on the dresser mirror in pink lipstick: "GOODBYE BUDDHA!"

Ted drank the drink, put the glass down and saw himself in the mirror—very fat, very old. He had no idea what to do next.

He carried the Cutty Sark back to the bed, sat down heavily on the edge of the mattress where he and Victoria had sat together. He lifted the bottle and sucked at it as the bright neon lights from the boulevard came through the dusty blinds.

He sat, looking out, not moving, watching the cars passing back and forth.

Photo: Richard Robinson

CHARLES BUKOWSKI is one of America's best-known contemporary writers of poetry and prose, and, many would claim, its most influential and imitated poet. He was born in Andernach, Germany, to an American soldier father and a German mother in 1920, and brought to the United States at the age of three. He was raised in Los Angeles and lived there for fifty years. He published his first story in 1944 when he was twenty-four and began writing poetry at the age of thirty-five. He died in San Pedro, California, on March 9, 1994, at the age of seventy-three, shortly after completing his last novel, *Pulp* (1994).

During his lifetime he published more than forty-five books of poetry and prose, including the novels *Post Office* (1971), *Factotum* (1975), *Women* (1978), *Ham on Rye* (1982), and *Hollywood* (1989). Among his most recent books are the posthumous editions of *What Matters Most Is How Well You Walk Through the Fire* (1999), *Open All Night: New Poems* (2000), *Beerspit Night and Cursing: The Correspondence of Charles Bukowski and Sheri Martinelli, 1960–1967* (2001), and *The Night Torn Mad with Footsteps: New Poems* (2001).

All of his books have now been published in translation in over a dozen languages and his worldwide popularity remains undiminished. In the years to come, Ecco will publish additional volumes of previously uncollected poetry and letters.